TIGRIS

CLARENCE COPELAND JR.

LITTLE PUBLISHING, LLC

Printed in the United States of America
First Printing 2021
First Edition 2021

ISBN: 978-1-7343314-6-2

10 9 8 7 6 5 4 3 2 1

TIGRIS

PREFACE

DESCRIPTION OF THE TIGERS IN TIGRIS

In this story, the tigers walk upright, and they have no tail. To walk on all fours is a special skill that these tigers do not possess. It has only been done once in the history of tigers, and it was done by king Shannon, the grandfather of Tigris. The average height for a male tiger is six feet four inches tall, and the average height for a female tiger is six feet two inches tall. All the tigers have a muscular build. Some are slim like volleyball players, and some are bulky like football players, but not too heavy. All tigers have the traditional colors of tigers. These colors are orange with black stripes or white with black or dark stripes like most tigers have. Over ninety percent of the tigers have yellow or blue eyes, but their eye color and shape depend upon the region they are from. Tigers from Erland Kingdom struggle to see in the light, while tigers from Arias Kingdom struggle to see in the dark.

Tigers from Erland Kingdom have bigger pupils than the tigers from Arias Kingdom. Some tigers have a small mane on the top of their heads and middle of the back, and the colors vary from blonde, black or brunette. The elders have gray manes. These tigers speak English, but some can speak other languages depending on the region they are from. All the tigers are athletic, some more athletic than others. They do not wear shoes. The adult tigers like to wear cloaks that are either black or gray, but if the adult is a member of the governing board, their cloaks can be green-blue or orange. The young tigers wear cloaks as well, but they wear shorts and shirts when they are playing or exercising. The young female tigers wear a dress from time to time. Most male tigers walk around with a sword strapped to their backs, while only a few of the female tigers have this privilege.

PROLOGUE

Tigelandia contains two different large kingdoms separated by a forest known as the Taiga forest. On one side of the forest is Arias Kingdom, where Tigris is from, and on the other side of the forest is Erland Kingdom, home of Tigeria.

Arias Kingdom is a beautiful and pristine Kingdom that has all four seasons. There are lakes, streams and mountains full of gold and silver. The jewels are visible from the land due to the clear water. Arias Kingdom also boasts of lakes filled with fish, shellfish, lobsters, crabs and other vital animals to the people of Arias Kingdom. The lakes provide approximately fifty percent of the food source to the inhabitants of the land. And the water that pours from the falls of Arias Kingdom contains the purest water in Tigelandia. The waterfall is where you can find most of the tigers playing on hot days. These waterfalls are extremely beautiful in the winter because they freeze up, capturing the landscape's beauty.

Arias Kingdom is a place where tigers who have survived previous battles chose to live with their families because King Shannon, the former ruler of the Arias Kingdom, welcomed all— even former enemies. The tigers who came were tired of fighting, and they only wanted peace. King Shannon was the best ruler and greatest warrior that the Arias Kingdom had ever seen. Standing seven feet tall with a muscular build, he reigned for more than twenty years. He wore long black dreadlocks that came down to his waist, and his eyes were a rare color of orange.

King Shannon was the only Tiger who defeated King Saber in battle. Arias Kingdom was the last kingdom to fall to King Saber. Often, King Saber sent a few of his soldiers to seek treasures and young tigresses from Arias Kingdom as part of a treaty signed by King Shannon to save his kingdom from slaughter. Sometimes this led to defiance, a mild disturbance.

Many of the tigers residing in Arias Kingdom were former fighters and very loyal to King Shannon.

King Shannon and his wife were poisoned by some of his most trusted guards who had been persuaded by King Saber. They both succumbed to death. Now the tigers from Kingdom Arias pledge their loyalty to Tylissa, daughter of King Shannon and Queen Mary.

Queen Mary was the wife of King Shannon. Queen Mary was a beautiful princess from a neighboring kingdom who met King Shannon when her father teamed up with King Shannon to fight against King Saber. Tylissa never claimed to be the ruler of Arias Kingdom. Still, she fell into the role by default, being the only child of King Shannon.

Once king Shannon died, Tylissa became the greatest warrior Arias Kingdom had, and she was a fierce protector of her kingdom. Tylissa was loved by all in her kingdom.

Erland Kingdom

Unlike Arias Kingdom, Erland Kingdom is a cold, dark and desolate place where the wind doesn't blow, and the soil is so hard that no edible plants can grow. In Tigerland, it rains a lot, and the kingdom experiences six months of darkness and six months of sun. Erland Kingdom drips in offensive odor, as it always has a stench of death—as rotten corpses litter the ground. Erland Kingdom's closest flowing river has fast running water, strong currents, and many boulders, so anything that falls into this river often meets its doom. This makes the river a very unreliable food source. It is nearly impossible to be nourished by the deadly waters. Most of the trees in Erland Kingdom are filled with dead leaves due to a lack of sunlight. Erland Kingdom has some mountains, but they are rugged and make traveling difficult. Erland Kingdom is filled with vultures; apart from that, there are not many other forms of animals. When the tigers of Erland Kingdom want to play in the water to cool off—they must travel to some of the smaller kingdoms they defeated to play in good water. Seventy-five percent of the treasures and other valuable resources the Erland Kingdom posses were acquired through fighting and slaughtering nearby kingdoms. There were many smaller kingdoms from nearby areas that were conquered by King Saber. One of King Saber's tactics: declare peace in the regions and invite members from other kingdoms over for a celebration and poison them all.

King Saber would also have some of his skilled fighters pretend to defect, only to get close enough to the leaders of other kingdoms and assassinate them by any means possible. After conquering many kingdoms, he would demand jewelry or the firstborn daughter from each couple who produced a child.

Erland Kingdom is only inhabited by tigers, and no humans live there because the tigers who live there eat humans. The Erland Kingdom trades jewels for human slaves who work extremely hard and make the humans breed constantly keep their stock of humans full.

The humans are used for building projects, gardening, servants and providing food for the tigers. Erland Kingdom is ruled by King Saber and his twin children, Tigeria and Razor.

CHAPTER 1

The sounds of the airplane wheels screech on the ground at Siem Reap International Airport in Northwest Cambodia. Clarence, a herpetologist from Miami, Florida, and a University of Miami graduate, wakes from a long nap. His presence is undeniable—a strong African American who stands six foot four inches tall, with broad shoulders, muscular arms and an athletic body. He sports a shaved head.

Clarence was born and raised in Miami, Florida, and he is the youngest of seven children. A former football and rugby player, he still plays flag football on the weekends. He lives with a former teammate he played football with during his college career. Clarence has five sisters, one brother. His hobbies include basketball, swimming and watching nature shows with his daughter. He has always been fascinated by animals and wildlife since he was a young kid. Interestingly, Clarence became interested in snakes after being bitten by one when he was a child.

Clarence is a single father of one child, a daughter named Deysia, age 12. Deysia's mom, Rosa, was from the Dominican Republic. Rosa died in a car crash when Deysia was two years old. Deysia is the leader of her girl scout troop. She loves nature and enjoys volunteering at animal shelters. Deysia has rabbits, birds and snakes that she cares for at her grandparents' house. Deysia also plays basketball and soccer for her middle school and is the team captain for both sports. Deysia wants to be a veterinarian because she wants to work with animals like her father.

Clarence went into a deep depression when he lost Rosa, and he was not mentally fit to raise a child on his own. Clarence thought it was best that Deysia lived with his parents until he became mentally stable.

Exiting the plane, Clarence met his tour guide, Boran, holding a sign with Clarence's name.

"Hey…I'm Clarence," he said, shaking Boran's hand.

"Hi," said Boran.

"What does Boran mean?" Clarence asked.

"My name means *ancient* in Cambodian language."

The two men loaded Clarence's luggage in Boran's small car.

"Hey! Am I going to fit in there?" asked Clarence, noticing the size of Baron's small black Toyota. The two men shared a laugh as they drove off.

"I'm headed to the town of Kampong Thom, near the *Prey Lang* Forest."

"What are you looking for there?" asked Boran.

"A specific kind of snake thought to be extinct."

"You are going into the forest?" asked Boran.

"Well," said Clarence sarcastically, "That's where most snakes are."

"Be safe in the forest because there is a war going on," warned Boran.

"Is the military fighting another country?"

"No," Boran replied.

"Do you know what you're getting into?" Boran asked Clarence.

"No," he replied.

Boran and Clarence arrived at the hotel where Clarence was going to be staying for his expedition. Once they unloaded, Boran closed the trunk, and Clarence paid him while also passing a business card.

"By the way," said Clarence. "Who's at war?"

"You'll never believe me," replied Boran.

Clarence checked into the hotel and took his luggage to the room. He opened the door and laughed when he saw the bed because it was small along with everything else. Clarence unpacked his bags and set out his gear for his trip to the forest tomorrow.

Clarence awoke the next day feeling refreshed. He packed his camping gear and headed for the receptionist desk so they could call him a cab.

"Taxi will be here in twenty minutes," said the clerk. "You can wait outside."

"Thanks," said Clarence, collecting his gear and heading to the curb.

CHAPTER 2

The sounds of the bushes and branches crackled and snapped, followed by silence and the subsequent squealing of a boar. The noise stopped. Tylissa, daughter of King Shannon and Queen Mary, stood up with blood dripping from her claws. Tylissa said to herself, "Either my prey is getting faster, or I am getting slower."

Tylissa became ruler of Arias Kingdom when her parents passed away. Tylissa is the bravest and the most skilled fighter in her village. She fought in many battles and was clearly the best fighter (male or female) that anyone in her village had seen, apart from her father, King Shannon.

Tylissa has earned many awards and achievements for her willingness to risk life and limb to protect her village. Tylissa stands six feet, three inches tall. Her mane is blonde and her eyes blue. Tylissa has a muscular build, and her legs are one of the first things you notice when you see her. Tylissa never wanted the title of Queen, but she understands that she is the protector of her village, and some of the elder tigers still call her Queen Tylissa. She is single with no offspring. Tylissa is the keeper of peace in her village. Some of her hobbies include gymnastics, gardening, swimming, wrestling and mastering weapons. Tylissa is very crafty with the way she uses her swords, staff and bow and arrows during war, so she constantly trains when she has time. After she made her kill, she thought she overheard someone crying. She moved some bushes out of the way and could see a young Tigress crying. Tylissa found this strange because most of the young tigers weren't permitted to play alone in the forest. Suddenly, Tylissa realized that this young tigress wasn't from her kingdom.

"Are you lost?" she asked the little girl. The girl nodded yes.

Tylissa reached out her hand, and everything went dark.

~   ~   ~

Clarence asked the driver to take him to the Prey Lang Forest.

"I can take you close to the forest…but you'll have to walk about a mile the rest of the way."

"No problem," he said, "but why can't you enter the forest? Are you afraid?"

"No human goes to the forest because those that do rarely make it out."

"What happens to the people that enter the forest?"

"There are things that happen in the forest we don't discuss."

Upon hearing that, Clarence looked worried for the first time. He put all the gear he had in his backpack, and he started his hike. As Clarence got near the center of the forest, he could catch a king cobra, three black mambas and one green mamba. These were some of the most poisonous snakes in the world. Clarence came to find a certain species of snakes that belong to the Krait family, like a Malayan Krait, Banded Krait and a Red Headed Krait, but they were exceedingly difficult to locate. When Clarence did find snakes, he took blood samples, and he measured and weighed the snakes as well. As Clarence continued his search in the forest, he heard someone moaning.

"Hello?!" he called out.

"Help!" the voice cried back.

Cautiously, Clarence went deeper into the forest and saw what he thought was a Tiger. He was blown away by the visual because *this* was no ordinary tiger! This tiger had female human body parts. Suddenly, the tigress spotted Clarence and asked, "Can you please help me?"

Clarence was shocked because, to his knowledge, no tiger has ever talked! For several moments, he was stunned into silence.

"Well..." she snapped. "Can you?"

It was then that Clarence noticed she was bleeding from her abdomen. Slowly, he approached. Upon reaching her, he took some gauze out of his backpack and pressed it against her slashed wound.

"Do you have a name?" he asked curiously.

"Tylissa," she said.

"I'm Clarence."

"What kind of name is that?" she asked.

"European, I believe…" he replied.

Tylissa explained that she stopped to help a younger female tigress who asked her for directions, but before she could give directions, she was struck in the head. "I think it was a planned attack," she confirmed. Clarence offered her water along with pain pills. "What are these white circle things?" Tylissa asked, looking at the pills.

"They'll help you with the pain," said Clarence.

Tylissa swallowed the pills down with water, and after a couple of minutes passed, Clarence reached out his hand and asked, "Can you stand?" She accepted, standing up. Clarence's jaw dropped as she was the same height as he was.

"What's wrong?" she asked innocently.

"I wasn't aware tigers could talk, let alone stand upright or walk," Tylissa said she could get back to her kingdom on her own, but Clarence insisted on helping her.

"It's not a good idea," she said. Then suddenly, she fell backward, and Clarence grabbed her arm to help her stand back up. "You need help," said Clarence. "Where do you live?"

"Okay," she said, agreeing to let him help…but she knew it was dangerous. But there was no other option.

Clarence could see that she was in a lot of pain, so he put his backpack in the bush, then he put her on his back. Good thing he was so strong because she was a hefty size package to carry for sure!

CHAPTER 3

After carrying Tylissa for two miles, Clarence came to a heavily dense spot in the forest.

"Keep going," she said.

"But the trail ended," he protested.

"Okay," she said, "please put me down." He did softly, but she still grimaced in pain while holding her stomach. Tylissa went into the bush where the trail had ended.

"Follow me," she directed. Tylissa took about twenty steps, then parted the bushes with her hand. Clarence's eyes grew large as he was amazed to see such a beautiful sight.

"This is my kingdom…Arias Kingdom."

As Clarence proceeded to walk, he was amazed to see beautiful mountains, lakes and streams that were clear as day. Suddenly, he was approached by two large Tigers wielding swords in his direction. Clarence backed up and fell to the ground, but before the swords made contact, Tylissa blocked them with her left arm and said, "He's with me."

The two Tigers growled with disgust before asking Tylissa, "What happened?"

"I was attacked while helping a young tigress. I believe it was a setup."

Clarence was in awe and equally shocked by another "talking tiger." He was also stunned by the size of them. The male tigers stood about six feet eight inches tall. Tylissa held out her hand to help Clarence get back to his feet.

"It looks like you have all the help you need, so can you point me in the direction I need to go?"

"Don't leave," she said. "You're welcome to stay the night."

Clarence to thought himself, this is all weird to me, but replied with, "I have to get back to my studies."

"There are dangers in the forest that you're not aware of. I can show you in the morning and guide you out of the forest safely."

"Okay, I'll stay…" he agreed.

This made Tylissa happy, and she smiled.

The two of them walked back to her residence, but the guards kept a close eye on Clarence. He drew suspicion as there were no humans in the village with his size, color and physique.

When Tylissa and Clarence arrived at her residence. Tylissa has a one-story two-bedroom villa located in the center of the village. She has a garden out front where she grows tomatoes, carrots and red peppers. The inside of her house is beautifully decorated with flowers and plants hanging inside her residence. The living room is full of trophies and plaques she won from various competitions in the village and her battles in war. She also had swords and knives hanging on the wall and over the fireplace is a picture of her parents, King Shannon and Queen Mary.

Tylissa sat down on her couch.

"How are you feeling?" Clarence asked her.

"The pain is coming back."

"Do you have a needle and thread?" he asked.

"No," she replied.

"I have some medical equipment in my backpack."

Tylissa called the two guards into her residence. Tylissa asked them would they go and retrieve the backpack that belonged to Clarence? The guards agreed, and Tylissa gave them the location where the backpack was placed.

Clarence sat near Tylissa on the couch. Tylissa could see the confusion on Clarence's face.

"Are you okay?" she asked.

Clarence paused for a couple of seconds and said, "I feel like I'm in a dream and can't wake up."

"It's not a dream. In fact, there's a war going on between Arias Kingdom and the kingdom of Erland Kingdom."

"Are there other tigers out here like yourself?" Clarence asked.

"Yes…there are others like me."

"There has never been an outsider that has known about the kingdoms in Tigelandia." Tylissa looked Clarence into his eyes and said, "I would like you to keep it a secret…do you understand?" "I'm not going to say anything," Clarence said.

Tylissa began to tell Clarence the story of her Kingdom and her world, explaining, "There were more kingdoms, but they were conquered and decimated by Erland Kingdom, and their ruler was the one responsible for my parent's death, "I'm sorry to hear about your parents," said Clarence. "I have a question for you…has your kind always been around?" Clarence asked.

"What do you mean…my kind?" with a hint of anger in her voice. "Tigers that talk and walk upright," he stated for clarity. "Yes," she responded. "For at least a century or more. "Our village comes under attack every so often, but lately, nothing major has taken place." "And that's why you didn't want me to go into the forest alone?" Clarence asked. "They eat humans in Erland Kingdom." "I thought that's what tigers were supposed to do!" he said with a chuckle. "But seriously, thank you for warning me." The guards eventually returned with Clarence's backpack.

"Are you hungry?"

"Yes," he said.

Tylissa tried to stand but was in too much pain. Clarence said, "Just tell me what you have, and I can prepare it. Clarence prepared some deer meat along with vegetables. The two sat at the table enjoying themselves with conversation and a little flirting, mainly by

Tylissa. She grabbed Clarence's arm when he served her and asked Clarence if he ate tiger meat. She winked, which drew a chuckle from Clarence. After dinner and hygiene, Clarence asked Tylissa to lay flat on the couch so he could look at her wound. When Clarence took off the gauze, he noticed the wound was already starting to heal. "Wow!" he said, "I've never seen a wound heal so fast." Tylissa smiled.

"Is that funny?"

"I'm laughing at you!" she said.

"Why? What did I do?"

"I saw you checking out my bosom and other body parts."

"Please forgive me," he said, embarrassed. "I don't mind...I actually like it," Tylissa said. Clarence stitched up the wound that Tylissa had on her abdomen and gave her two more aspirin. Clarence re-wrapped the wound then they prepared for bed. Tylissa hugged Clarence, thanked him for all his work, and then told him he had to sleep on the couch. The next day, Tylissa awakened with a smile on her face. She couldn't wait to see Clarence. When she got to the couch, she saw that Clarence was gone. She searched for him through the house then she went to look outside, but did not find him. Tylissa noticed Clarence had left some of his belongings, so she gathered them up and put them in a small pouch. Later that day, Tylissa went to the forest, hoping to find Clarence in the same area they had first encountered each other. Once in the area, she picked up on Clarence's scent. When she spotted Clarence, she started to stalk him like he was prey, following his every move. Tylissa was able to make it to a tree that was right above Clarence's workstation he had set up to document his findings. After Clarence was done weighing, taking blood and pictures of a king cobra he caught—he released it back in the forest. Clarence was about to pack his bags when Tylissa jumped out of the tree and landed on his back, and said, "I gotcha!" Clarence quickly rolled over and saw Tylissa under him between his legs smiling.

"What are you doing here?" Clarence asked.

"Hunting my prey," Tylissa said as she kissed Clarence on the lips.

Clarence was shocked, but he did not show any reaction to the kiss, so he stood up, helped Tylissa up, and went back to his studies. "What are you doing messing with poisonous snakes?" Clarence tried to ignore Tylissa as he continued documenting his work in his journal, but he couldn't help himself as he stared at Tylissa's erect nipples poking through her cloak.

"This is my job," he said, then began taking blood, venom and scales from the captured snakes before letting them free. Clarence began more documentation but became distracted when he saw Tylissa breast hanging out of her cloak. "The snakes are very dangerous to humans but not tigers," she said. Clarence dropped the pen he was holding and turned to face Tylissa.

"Tigers are immune to poisonous snakes?" he asked in disbelief. "Yes," Tylissa nodded. "And trying to avoid looking at me could also be dangerous," she said with a wink.

"Is that right?" he asked.

"It only makes me want you more."

Clarence tried to ignore what she said, so he asked her, "Where did you come from?"

"My kingdom."

"I know that, but I didn't see or hear you."

"That was the plan," she said. "You left some belongings," she said, giving him the pouch—she was holding. Clarence thanked her for returning his items. Clarence and Tylissa locked eyes as they could both feel a deep passion for each other.

"I'm happy to see you," said Clarence.

"Likewise," she replied.

The two of them chatted for another thirty minutes before Clarence had to leave because he remembered what she had said about the Tigers eating people. Clarence gave Tylissa a hug and a kiss on the cheek. Then he apologized to Tylissa for kissing her. Tylissa grabbed Clarence and said, "It's about time you make a move." The two embraced as they locked lips for about twenty seconds. Clarence was swept off his feet immediately.

"Wait…" he staggered, "What just happened?"

"Nature just happened," she laughed. The two let go of the embrace, and they headed their separate ways. Tylissa was still in awe and didn't want her time with Clarence to end, but unfortunately, the time was over.

Later that evening, Clarence was writing in his journal documenting information about the snakes he had caught. Suddenly, he heard what he thought was a thud on the window, but he paid it no attention and went back to writing. Clarence heard the thud again and went to check it out, opening the sliding glass door to his hotel room balcony. He was amazed when he saw Tylissa standing there dressed in an all-black cloak. Clarence quickly motioned for Tylissa to come up, and in one leap, she jumped onto the second-floor balcony. Clarence shook his head in disbelief, then brought her inside and asked, "Are you crazy? How did you find me?"

"You do know tigers have a great sense of smell, right?"

"You shouldn't be in public."

"I was careful not to be seen."

Clarence started to ask her what she was doing here, but before he could finish, she put her finger to his lips and said, "I am here with you, and you want to ask questions?" The two embraced and started to kiss. After the kissing stopped, Clarence paused for a second then said, "I have never been with a tigress or an animal."

"Hold on tight because I am ready to go all night," she said.

She picked Clarence up and threw him on the bed. She ripped his clothes off and began to lick Clarence from head to toe. Before Clarence could react, Tylissa put his penis inside of her. She started riding him up and down. The bed frame was about to break from the constant pounding. Tylissa put both of her hands behind Clarence's neck to hold him tight as she was about to orgasm. Clarence noticed she was roaring softly, but he knew that a loud roar was coming, so he put his hand over her mouth, and soon as he did, Tylissa let out a roar that was louder than any roar Clarence had ever heard. Her claws sank into Clarence's back, clawing him deeply, causing bruising and bleeding. She licked Clarence's face and neck after she orgasmed, then collapsed on his chest. Clarence was confused, not knowing what just happened. He had never had such good sex in his whole life. He kissed Tylissa and said, "thank you."

Tylissa responded, "I am in heat."

"That was the best sex ever," said Clarence.

Tylissa said, "Round two..." and she mounted Clarence for another round of hot steamy sex. Clarence was powerless. This was different for him having someone that wasn't human. But he enjoyed it. He also liked the fact that someone else took control in the bedroom. They made love at least four more times throughout the night.

CHAPTER 4

Later that evening, Clarence called his taxi driver, Boran, to take him to the forest. Boran picked Clarence up at the hotel at 6pm. When they arrived at the forest, Boran told Clarence, "Be careful."

"I will," said Clarence.

"What time do you need to be picked up?" Boran asked.

"I'll call you in two hours," Clarence said.

Clarence exited the vehicle and entered the forest. Boran said a small prayer for Clarence then he left. Clarence followed the path he did the first time he entered the forest. With his flashlight in hand, he started to head towards Tigelandia. He was about a mile away when he heard a noise that sounded like footsteps hitting the ground. He turned and looked behind him, but there was nothing there. Clarence kept walking, and he heard the sound again. He grabbed a pocketknife out of his right pocket and said, "Who is there?" He heard the footsteps get louder and faster coming towards him.

Clarence took off running, and when he glanced back, he saw a boar that was at least three feet tall with fangs six inches long, charging at him. Clarence ran faster and faster. Suddenly, he heard a pig squealing. He turned around again and was no longer being chased. He stopped to catch his breath and said aloud, "What the hell was that?"

A familiar voice said, "That's dinner."

The carcass of the boar dropped from above and landed near his feet. He looked up and saw Tylissa. Clarence was so happy to see her. She jumped from the tree to the ground, then into Clarence's arm as they started to kiss. Clarence said, "I am so happy to see you."

"Oh yeah?" Tylissa teased, "What took you so long?"

Clarence kissed her and said, "I was waiting for the sun to go down."

Tylissa said, "I have been waiting for you for hours."

The two embraced and kissed again. Tylissa grabbed the boar with ease and said, "Let us go eat." At home, Tylissa began to cut the carcass into smaller pieces.

"How did you kill the boar?" Clarence asked Tylissa. Tylissa held up her hands, showing her claws and smiled. He shook his head and said, "I have marks all over my body from those claws."

Tylissa smiled and said, "Not guilty," as she stuck her tongue between her claws in a flirtatious manner. The two of them enjoyed dinner and wine, then they both participated in the clean-up together. After cleaning, they sat on the couch, holding each other.

Clarence asked Tylissa her opinion about the two of them. Tylissa said, "I love you a lot."

"I love you too," said Clarence. "But humans aren't welcome here. Has there ever been a relationship between a tiger and a human?"

Tylissa said, "No...because that kind of relationship is forbidden."

Tylissa said, "I am sorry to say this, but humans are only used for hard labor and food in most villages."

Clarence took a big gulp and said, "Well...that's not what I wanted to hear." Tylissa grabbed Clarence and said, "Don't worry...I am sure we will figure something out."

The two of them went to bed and made passionate love throughout the night. The next morning Tylissa awakened and noticed that Clarence had left. She went to the living room to find him, but he was not there. She looked around the house, but again she didn't see him, so she began to panic. She looked out back and saw Clarence sitting down alone.

"My love...is everything well?" Tylissa asked.

"Everything is fine," said Clarence.

"Please be honest," said Tylissa.

"I may have to leave and return to my country soon because funding for the snake project is about to end."

"You mean leave and never come back?" Tylissa asked.

Clarence nodded yes, and she ran into the house and began to cry. Clarence followed her inside, and he held her and told her things were going to be fine.

"How can you say that when you are leaving me?"

"I was sent here on a job, and I never thought I would fall in love…let alone fall in love with someone that was not a human." Tylissa cried harder and told Clarence the best thing for him to do is leave now. She opened the door, hoping to usher him out.

"Please listen to me," said Clarence.

"Get out now before you regret it!" she shouted, holding up her claws!! Clarence grabbed his belongings and left, and Tylissa slammed the door behind him.

Later that evening, Clarence was all packed as he sat in the lobby waiting for his ride to the airport. He shed tears thinking about Tylissa, but he knew he had to leave. Around 7 p.m., Tylissa showed up at the hotel where Clarence was staying. She hoped to see him one last time. So again, she threw rocks several times, hitting the window, but this time—it was a European couple who came to the window. The husband shouted, "Hey, you freak! Get away from here!"

Tylissa took off running towards the forest. She felt defeated and ashamed as tears ran down her face. Tylissa made it to the forest, then found a tree and sat up against it. After a couple of minutes of sitting and crying, flowers started to fall on her lap. At first, she ignored it because she was hurt, but the flowers kept falling on her. Tylissa stood up and looked in the tree to see Clarence just standing there smiling.

Tylissa's eyes filled with tears of joy. Clarence jumped down and asked, "What took you so long?"

The two of them laughed and kissed while holding each other closely. Clarence said, "Let's go home…"

Tylissa smiled and said, "Yes, my love."

When they got home, Clarence held Tylissa close, and he asked, "What about the villagers?" Tylissa said she would meet with the village elders and explain everything to them tomorrow. Clarence said, "That would be great." He leaned in for a kiss, and Tylissa asked, "How do you feel about being with an animal?" Clarence's eyes got big because he never thought of it that way. He said, "Well, at first, it all seemed like a terrible dream that was happening, but then the dream became something that has been missing in my life."

"What's that?" Tylissa asked.

"Love," said Clarence. "I'm missing love. I've been single for over ten years because I have only focused on my job and battled with depression. I never took time to enjoy the things that were important to me."

"I understand," Tylissa said.

"How do you feel about me being with a human?" Tylissa said, "I never had an opinion about them. I only agreed that no one in this village would cause them harm or eat them."

"Well, I am glad to hear that," and they smiled and kissed each other. Tylissa started walking towards the bedroom when Clarence jumped on her back, gently biting her neck. Tylissa carried Clarence to the bed. Clarence got off her back as he ripped up her cloak, taking it off her body. Clarence laid Tylissa back on the bed and opened her legs. He said, "Now I am the hunter, and you are the prey."

Tylissa's body squirmed in pleasure as Clarence started licking her between her legs. Tylissa screamed in pleasure, "What are you doing to me?"

Clarence said, "We call it oral sex in my country. Do you want me to stop?"

Tylissa grabbed the back of Clarence's neck and said, "Only if you want to die."

She started grinding her vagina on Clarence's face, then she roared loud as she orgasmed in his mouth. Clarence turned her around and said, "We call this position doggy style."

Tylissa said, "you call it…" but before she could finish, Clarence inserted his penis into her wet vagina, and she collapsed from the pleasure. Clarence pounded Tylissa hard, and she enjoyed every inch and minute of her being pounded. He laid her flat on her stomach and licked her neck as he thrust her harder and deeper, causing them both to orgasm and roar at the same time, then he collapsed on top of her. The two of them laid there breathing heavy and sweating profusely. Tylissa said, "When I get my energy back, you are in trouble." The two of them both laughed, then went to bed.

The next day Tylissa met with the village elders. She really didn't need their approval, but as the leader of her village, she knew it was important to explain her decision. Tylissa asked the elders how they felt about her having a relationship with a human? John, the oldest Tiger in the village, was seventy years old and wore glasses. He walked with a cane, and his mane was gray. John had fought for both villages at one time in his life, but it was King Shannon who gave him his freedom. John said, "My dear…you know such a relationship is forbidden," while adjusting his eyeglasses. Tylissa let them know that Clarence found her in the forest, and he saved her life by stopping the bleeding, and if not for him, she would be dead. John asked Tylissa how she could assure them that he will keep their existence a secret? Tylissa said, "He has vowed to keep everything a secret, and he has vowed to help the village as much as possible." One elder jokingly asked, "Did you think about having Clarence move in?" All the other tigers giggled. Tylissa said, "Yes…and do you have a problem with that?" as she looked at the tiger who made the comment with a look that could kill. The room went silent, and the elder tiger who made the comment bowed his head. Tylissa asked, "Are there any more questions?"

All the elders looked at each other and said, "No questions…" but an older female tiger said, "I will not give my approval on something like this." Some of the other elders agreed with her. John excused all the other elder tigers. They shook Tylissa's hand and kissed her cheek before they left the room. John asked Tylissa to stay behind, and once the others cleared out, he told Tylissa that he trusts her opinion. John said, "I want to know if you love him."

"With all my heart," said Tylissa.

"I needed to hear you say that," said John.

John let Tylissa know that he will speak with the other leaders to see if he could get their approval. She hugged and thanked John, then kissed him on the cheek. Tylissa entered the house, and she told

Clarence the good news. Clarence hugged Tylissa and said, "I was so worried." He asked Tylissa to have a seat then he grabbed her hand. Clarence told Tylissa that he had a daughter back in his country, and it wouldn't be a good idea to bring her to Arias Kingdom. Tylissa became upset because she didn't want to lose Clarence but understood the situation with Clarence and his daughter. Clarence told Tylissa not to cry and reassured her, "We will make this happen."

Clarence used his satellite phone to call his friend and roommate, Mark, back home in Miami. Mark was a former football teammate of Clarence when they played football. Mark and Clarence both played the linebacker position. Mark is Caucasian with sandy blonde hair and stands 6'2. Mark is single with no kids, but he helped Clarence with his daughter, Deysia, after she lost her mother. Deysia calls Mark "Uncle Mark." Clarence told Mark that he is moving to Cambodia.

"Tell me her name," Mark said while laughing.

Clarence chuckled and replied, "You wouldn't believe me if I told you." Mark said, "I have been drinking, so try me."

"I will tell you when I return."

Clarence asked Mark to start packing up some of his items, and Mark said, "I will do that for you."

Clarence thanked Mark for helping him. Clarence phoned his parents and let them know he would be home in a couple of days with some important news. Afterward, Clarence called Boran to schedule a noon pick-up for tomorrow. Clarence went inside to let

Tylissa know that his ride will be there tomorrow. Tylissa hugged and kissed Clarence and asked, "You are coming back, right?"

"Yes, my love…but I must take care of some business back home." Clarence let her know that he needed to speak with his daughter, family and employer.

"Try not to take too long."

"Why not?" Clarence asked.

"I'm pregnant," said Tylissa.

"You're pregnant? Is that possible?"

"I'm not sure, but something is growing inside of me." Clarence was stunned into silence.

"Well…" he said, "That gives me six to eight months before you have the baby."

"I'm not human, and we deliver in three to four months. Clarence was confused, and he said, "three months." Tylissa said yes. Clarence knew that he had to hurry and get back soon.

"Tell me about your daughter?" said Tylissa.

"Deysia is my whole world, but I do not wish to talk about her now," said Clarence. He knew how devastated he and his daughter would be without each other. After a long flight, Clarence returned home to Miami, Florida. He called his parents, brother and sisters to let them know that he landed safely. Clarence went to sleep because he had a lot of running around to do the next couple of days.

Upon returning home, he went to the University of Miami Campus and turned in all of the work he had conducted in

Cambodia, and he handed in his two weeks' notice to his supervisor. Clarence's supervisor asked him if everything was well, and Clarence stated yes. The supervisor let Clarence know if he ever needed a job, he could come back, and Clarence shook his hand, thanking him.

Later that day, Clarence met Mark at a local bar for a beer. Mark asked Clarence how he would tell his daughter he was moving away for a woman without her.

"I have no idea, but I feel like a coward for leaving my daughter to chase love."

"This lady must be one fine human being."

"What if I told you that I am not in love with a human?"

Mark looked confused and said, "if not a human...is it an animal?"

Clarence said, "Yes..." then shared that she was the most incredible woman he has ever met, but she just happens to be a "tigress." Again, Mark was confused and said, "Man...I think I've been drinking too much."

"I'm in love with a tiger."

Mark said, "Well...I thought it was sakes that you like the most.

"This is a female tiger who talks."

Mark spat out his beer and said, "What???"

"I know it sounds crazy, but you will find it hard to believe me."

"You are right because no one in the world would believe you."

"What man in his right mind would leave his family for an animal?"

"Clarence said just drop the conversation."

The next day Clarence picked up his daughter Deysia from school, and they went to have lunch. He explained to Deysia that he met a woman and fell in love. Deysia said, "That's great, dad!"

"Well…she lives in Cambodia, and I am going to move there."

"Oh wow!" said Deysia. "I'm excited to be moving out of the country."

"Well…my love…I will be going alone."

"What do you mean alone?" she asked. "And when are you coming back?"

Clarence stated, "I have no plans on coming back." As expected, Deysia cried and begged her father not to go, but Clarence had his mind made up. He hugged his daughter and promised her things would be better and that he would return to visit her soon.

"How is this fair for me that my mother and father leave me at my young age?"

They both shed tears, then embraced. Clarence continued to apologize to his daughter and said he was sorry and that he loved her.

Later that evening, Clarence returned to his parents' house, where his family threw a party for him and wished him well on his new adventures. Deysia stayed in her room, still angry at her father. His parents asked him if he thought he was making the right decision?

Clarence told his parents that he was in love with an incredible woman and he's not going to wait.

"Clarence's mom said, When can we meet this incredible woman?"

"Soon," he said to his mother.

After the party was over, Clarence hugged his sister and brother, and they wished him well. Clarence gave his daughter Deysia a big stuffed tiger and told her to never forget him. Deysia was crying, but she still grabbed the stuffed animal then kissed her dad goodbye. Clarence asked Mark to watch over his princess, and Mark said, "I will as if she was my own and please be safe."

Clarence returned to Cambodia and went to Village Arias to be with the love of his life, Tylissa. Two months after Clarence returned, Tylissa gave birth to a beautiful female tiger/human cub. They named her Tigris.

Chapter 5

Tigris is a 16-year-old female tigress, half-human and half tiger. When she was born, it was apparent to her parents that she was different from the other tigers in her village. Her face has human characteristics, which is the opposite of the rest of the tigers in her village. While most tigers have fur that covers their whole body, Tigris has fur on her backside, and smooth skin like a human's on her front side. Nevertheless, she was a beautiful baby tigress, and she was big for her size. Her father, Clarence, was accustomed to seeing babies between seven to nine pounds, but Tigris was a tall baby that weighed twenty pounds at birth. From the beginning, Clarence and Tylissa decided they would try to keep her a secret until the villagers accepted a human and tiger relationship completely. Tigris began walking one month after birth.

As a child, Tigris loved running through the house chasing after her father and mother whenever they played with her. Clarence could see the athleticism in his daughter because he and Tylissa were great athletes themselves. Her parents would cover Tigris whenever they went out in public. When Tigris was three, her parents started taking her to the forest to play so she could burn off energy because she was very active; and with her size and her adrenaline, she kept breaking statues and furniture around the house. Tigris loved to chase the animals and play with them in the forest. She was especially close to the sun bears. Tigris loved the way the sun bears moved through the trees with effort, and she would mimic this behavior. Whenever Tylissa wanted to cook rabbit for dinner, she would turn Tigris loose in the forest, and she would return with five or six rabbits in her mouth. At age seven, all the male and female tigers had to join the military academy. Tigris's parents were reluctant at first, but they knew it was necessary for her to learn how to fight in battle. By the time Tigris started the military academy, she was incredibly beautiful, tall, athletic, and very curvaceous. Tigris had brown/orange eyes and long, beautiful, dark dreadlocks that extend to the middle of her back. As a young woman, Tigris stood 6'6 with very muscular legs. During the academy, Tigris stood out with her looks, athleticism and her intelligence. Tigris was bigger than all of the other female tigers in school. She was made fun of by the male tigers, but they knew to keep their distance. They called her human child and man tiger. This made Tigris terribly upset, but she chose not to react with violence. Instead, when it came to combat drills, she took her frustration out by defeating the male tigers in all the athletic competitions that took place in training. Tigris excelled in military school by always coming in first with her education projects and physical drills.

During military competitions, Tigris had to compete with the male tigers because she was too big and strong for the female tigers in her class. Tigris graduated from the military academy at fifteen.

Although Tigris had both female and male friends, she was still lonely because it was hard to fit in with her looks. Male tigers were intimidated by her good looks and size, so many chose not to approach her. Tigris always thought something was wrong with herself. Tigris started liking the female tigers more because they were nice to her, and they never called her names or made fun of the way she looked. But she also liked male tigers but would just never tell them. Tylissa and Clarence didn't allow Tigris to go to friends' houses because they feared she'd be mistreated. So, Tigris spent most of her time in the forest with her animal friends, where she knew they would not judge her. She learned how to communicate with sun bears, cheetahs, rabbits, crocodiles and some of the other creatures in the forest. When she got older, she stopped eating the smaller animals because they had become her friends; however, she understood some of the bigger animals had to be used for dinner. Tigris number one forest friends were sun bears.

She loved to race them and challenge them in obstacle courses that were set up throughout the forest. Tigris loved everything about nature, and eventually, she found herself being a defender of nature, helping all the animals of the forest get along. When the animals had a dispute amongst themselves, it was Tigris they went to for her opinion. Ultimately, she would make the final decision on who was right or wrong. Tigris also helped the relationship between animals and tigers become stronger by being a mediator between tigers and the forest creatures. Tigris wasn't a secret anymore, and she was accepted by the people of her village and became a favorite amongst the elders. She would do their shopping and help them with gardening and other projects around their houses.

Tigris really loved her parents because they were always by her side, and they have always defended her. Everyone in the village adopted Tigris as their own because she was incredibly unique and special. Tigris' hobbies included racing, jumping, swimming, gardening, climbing trees and spending time in the forest.

CHAPTER 6

On a nice cool Saturday morning, most of the young tigers were out playing in the field under the watchful eye of the adult tigers waiting for field day to begin. All the kids and adults looked forward to field day. During field day, all the teenage male and female tigers participate in fun and games to win small prizes, such as used military weapons and snacks. There was one game called "catch your snack" that all the tigers loved to play. The game focused on the participant's hand and eye coordination to sharpen their athletic skills. A group of rabbits would be released and whoever caught the most rabbits won the game. Carl, one of the military trainers, said, "I need a competitor." Carl was a healthy elder tiger who oversaw the physical fitness of the young tigers interested in joining the military. Carl was a former general of the military in Arias Kingdom. He likes to run for miles and never ate meat. His healthy lifestyle contributed to his overall great shape. Carl stood six feet four inches tall, and he was well known for defeating five tigers at once during battle without even getting touched. A voice out of the crowd shouted, "I want to try."

The voice was that of a female. The crowd stilled to silence as Tigris repeated, "I want to try."

"Go ahead, little one," Carl said to Tigris. Tigris stood up, and Carl said, "oh, you are not so little." Tigris asked her parents, Clarence and Tylissa, if she could participate, and they nodded their heads. One of the young male tigers said, "She is a boy, not a girl!" and the juvenile male tigers laughed. Tylissa and Clarence shot the young tigers a dirty look. The young male saw them looking at him, and he ran close to his parents. Tigris refused to get upset because she had already learned to block out the petty jokes as she heard them many times.

"What do I need to do?" Tigris asked Carl. Carl told Tigris she has to round up all the rabbits when they are let loose, and the person with the most rabbits wins. Tigris asked, "Just grab them with my hand or mouth?"

"It would be difficult to grab them with your mouth unless you are on the ground."

Tigris said she was ready, and one of the young male tigers blurted, "She is too big and clumsy...she will never be able to do it." Carl lifted the gate, and the rabbits took off. Tigris knowing her ability, let the rabbits get a good head start, and one of the female tigers said, "Hurry up before they get away." Clarence asked, "What are you waiting for?" Tigris winked at her father and smiled. It looked like a track meet because all the rabbits were side by side, running in a straight line. When it appeared the rabbits were running in formation, Tigris took off—unlike the other tigers who had started off in the traditional way of running. Tigris leaped about twenty feet before she hit the ground running. The crowd gasped in amazement as she landed and quickly picked up speed. The crowd could see the power her legs were generating.

"Wow!" said Carl. "Look at that girl move."

Tigris caught up with the rabbits in no time. She leaned over and grabbed all the rabbits with one scoop of her paws, which were bigger than most male tigers in the village. All the tigers in attendance were amazed at her skills, even the elders.

"Did you see that?" Clarence asked Tylissa.

"Yes," Tylissa said. "That was incredible."

Some of the young male tigers who had picked on her from time to time began to cheer. Tigris returned with the rabbits and presented them to Carl. He was scratching his head before asking her, "Where did you learn how to run?"

Tigris threw her hands up and said, "I have no clue."

Carl let Tigris know that the rabbits belonged to her to eat. Tigris gave Carl a sad look and said, "Eat…no way!"

Carl said, "Most winners eat the rabbits they catch." Tigris felt disgusted and said, "okay," and left the field. She made eye contact with her parents and pointed towards the forest to ask her parents for permission to go to the forest. Clarence and Tylissa said, "Yes."

Clarence said, "Try not to stay late."

Tigris walked the rabbits back to the forest, and she let them know through facial expressions that they were never in trouble. The rabbits smiled at Tigris, then took off into the forest. The leader of the sun bears was the oldest female that Tigris called momma.

Momma was the matriarch of her family. She was fifty years old with gray hair over most of her body. Momma signaled by hand to Tigris that she did well, but she looked a little slow. Tigris jumped fifteen feet into the air, landing on the tree branch where momma was sitting. Tigris hugged momma as they shared a laugh. Tigris asked momma where the rest of the chimp crew were? Momma pointed towards the middle of the forest. Tigris tried to slowly ease in the direction where momma had pointed to get a head start, but momma knew what Tigris was trying to do. Before you knew it, the race was on. Some of the animals that were new to the forest would often mistake Tigris for an oversized sun bear because she moved through the trees and the brushes fluently. As good as Tigris was, she was no match for momma.

Tigris exited the tree with a backward somersault, landing on both feet. All the sun bears gave a small clap as they walked towards Tigris and started to groom her as if she were one of their own. Markey was a young chimp who was infatuated with the beauty of Tigris and her sexuality. Markey signaled to Tigris that she was a showoff, which caused an eruption of laughter from both the sun bears and Tigris. Tigris kissed Markey on the cheek, and he blushed and started wiping his cheek as if he hated the kiss. Tigris spent a lot of time with the sun bears and all the other animals in the forest she knew. Tigris would join the other animals in an opening in the forest called Tiger's Eye. This is where all the animals could drink while also playing in the water, and if Tigris were there because she had a special bond with all crocodiles in the river. Most of the bigger animals went there to get parasites removed from their skin.

Tigris would play a game with the leopards and cheetahs. She would try to jump across the narrowest part of the river without landing in the water. Some of the youngest and healthiest leopards and cheetahs would make it, but not the young and the old ones. Then there was Tigris who never backed down from a challenge and would make it about twenty feet into the river, always coming up about five feet short of the river's edge. After having fun with all her friends, Tigris would hug and kiss them all before signaling until we meet, never forget that I love you. Tigris was escorted to the edge of the forest by her sun bear friends then she would head for home.

CHAPTER 7

Tigeria and Razor are twin siblings. The twins were raised by their father, King Saber, the ruler of Erland Kingdom. King Saber is a large tiger who is from Siberia. He stands eight feet tall with black eyes and a dark brown mane, which was unusual for tigers to have. He got his name because he has two canine teeth that are seven inches long like a saber-toothed cat. King Saber is not muscular, but he is not obese. He was once married, but his wife died under suspicious circumstances. King Saber rules his kingdom with an iron fist. He is a great fighter who is very skilled with his five-foot sword. King Saber dominated his fights with brute strength. One of his methods of killing was to grab his victims by the throat, lift them off the ground then behead them with his five-foot-long sword. King Saber has also been known to use his canines to puncture his enemies' jugular veins and watch them bleed to death. His villagers respect him, but it is out of fear. King Saber participates in eating humans, but this practice was outlawed by many of the other Kingdoms. Nothing is approved without King Saber giving the final approval.

He is a grumpy tiger who hates almost everyone and everything. He was the executioner in his village at a young age. Currently, all crimes in his Kingdom are punished by beheading.

The twins lost their mother when they were one year old. The twins were mostly raised by older female tigers who King Saber hand-picked himself. The older tigresses were responsible for giving the twins everything they needed whenever they wanted it.

Since birth, Tigeria and Razor always competed with one another, no matter how large or small the task was. The two of them could be doing anything like chores, eating, swimming, laundry, etc. No matter the situation, they always found a way to make things competitive. They were always together and did everything together. One could even say they were inseparable. When they reached their teen years, they started doing their own thing.

Tigeria was tall and beautiful. She stood 6'4. Her body was slim, and she had large breasts with a curvy butt. She was the sexiest female tiger in all her village. She had a blonde mane, and her eyes were grayish and slanted. She was the opposite of her father and Razor, who both often used intimidation to gain respect. Tigeria was very calm and well-mannered for her age. She always said yes ma'am or no ma'am and yes sir and no sir when she spoke to adults in her village. Tigeria loved to fight with the male soldiers during battle drills. She always trained hard and was the only female from her village who fought in battles. Some of Tigeria's favorite hobbies included cooking, reading and dancing. She can often be heard in the castle singing and dancing in her room. Tigeria was also a big fan of nature.

She loved to go on picnics alone and just watch the animals in the forest. She loved to see how other creatures interacted in the wild.

Tigeria loved to swim and lay in the sun with no clothes on. This led to her having an audience of animals staring at her, but it only made her blush. She would draw the forest animals that she saw and would try to understand how they communicated.

Tigeria was a young girl trapped in a male-dominated society where women only had certain roles. By being in the military, she was trying to change the gender roles in her village and be an inspiration for younger female tigers. Tigeria struggled to have a good relationship with her father. The two of them often got into arguments about the way he treated her versus her brother. Tigeria also suffered from depression because she missed the mother/daughter bond that all females needed. She never accepted the fact that her mother was dead. Whenever she would ask about her mother, King Saber's story would always change—so this was one reason she grew suspicious of her mother's death and one of the reasons their father/daughter relationship wasn't the greatest. One thing that bothered Tigeria the most was it seemed as if her father could care less if his wife was gone. Tigeria isolated a lot. She would either be in her room, in the forest or training little female tigresses how to fight. This kept her busy so she could try to keep a positive mind. Male tigers would ask her out on dates, but her excuse was she had no time because she was busy. Almost everyone in her village loved her because she was very calm, respectful, helpful and nice.

Razor was quite different and never showed respect to adults. As a child, he was punished a lot for his behaviors, but his father, King

Saber, always let him get away with things. Razor stood 6'4. He had a dark, brown mane like his father, King Saber. Razor had one black eye and one blue eye. He was very muscular with enormous arms. Razor got his name from the six-inch claws, which were the biggest and sharpest throughout the Erland Kingdom. When Razor was younger, he did many wrongs because he knew no matter what he did, he would normally get away with it. At a young age, Razor ran with a younger crew of male tigers. They called themselves the "claw gang," and they were known for causing problems throughout the smaller villages they had already conquered.

The claw gang would demand jewels and other valuables from smaller villages without King Saber knowing. Razor liked to tell humans that they were free only to chase them down and kill them with one slash from his claws to the victim's neck. He would then return to his father and lie about how the human tried to escape, and he handled it—only to make himself look good in his father's eye. Razor was known for taking illicit substances that made him feel high and numb. He and the Claw Gang would be high for hours before they came back to reality. Razor had girlfriends, but he had also been rumored to engage in sexual activities with male tigers when he was high. His own villagers feared him because he had the support of King Saber, so most people stayed away from him. The older adult tigers complained about his behavior, but nothing was done. With all the bad things about Razor that were said, absolutely no one could complain about his fighting skills. When it came to training or competing, Razor was one hundred percent involved, and he always gave maximum effort. Therefore, many gave him a pass on his behavior because he was great at protecting the village. When Tigeria and Razor spent time together, they talked about their mother and what life might have been like with her around. Although the two of them had quite different lifestyles they, both felt the same way about their mother.

This was the only time Tigeria saw a different side of her brother Razor. Being twins, they shared a close bond and always supported each other. When they were younger, Razor always intervened when his sister and father begin to argue, always defending Tigeria, knowing that he would be punished—but he has his sister's back no matter what happens. So, they were often seen in the rain or late at night, doing extra physical drills for punishment or you can find them cleaning horse poop and washing the horses. The two always argued but were able to work out their differences by fighting with weapons but careful not to harm each other. Although Razor had the dominant personality, he always listened to his sister no matter the situation because he understood how hard things were for her being surrounded by male tigers most of her life. The twins had a bond that seemed unbreakable. One thing the twins both agreed upon was they never believed that their mother just left or died in a fatal accident. They have both approached their father with questions, but he always told a quick lie, or King Saber would ask them to get out of his presence. The twins always heard rumors about their mother's death, but all the people in the village feared King Saber so much that most of them refused to say a word. Nevertheless, the twins would try to get information from some of the older tigers, but they would only get bits and pieces of information. The twins were told the same story repeatedly about how their mom went swimming and drowned, never to be recovered. One-time, Tigeria asked King Saber if he knew the location for where her mother had allegedly drowned? The King became so furious with Tigeria that she would be confined to her room for two days. Razor once asked his father if he missed his wife. King Saber said, "Yes," and Razor asked, "Why are there are no pictures of mom in the house?"

King Saber walked up behind him and shoved him to the ground. The king told Razor to never come into his room again. The twins vowed that they would never stop trying to find their mother or, at minimum, the truth of what really happened to her.

CHAPTER 8

King Saber was talking with his son Razor about the amount of gold, silver, and other jewels they had saved. Razor let his father know that the supplies were running low, but King Saber had no idea Razor was going behind his back and giving the riches away to some of the tigresses he was dating. Razor also traded with neighboring villages for weapons and medicinal potions. Razor believed these potions gave him an advantage over his opponents during battle. Razor mentioned to his dad that it was time for another raid.

"I need to think about how things have been so peaceful," replied King Saber.

"We need to act now," said Razor, disagreeing with his father.

King Saber stomped his foot on the ground, and Razor jumped back.

"I make the decisions around here…now get out of my face!"

Razor went to talk to his sister, Tigeria, about going to Arias Kingdom.

"I'm willing to accompany you, but only if father approves."

Razor smirked in disgust.

After King Saber chatted with some of the elders, he decided to send Razor and Tigeria to Arias Kingdom—just to get a sample of what goods they had to offer. The next day Razor gathered up some of his loyal troops and told them to get prepared to ride out. Razor went to Tigeria's room and knocked on the door.

"Enter," said Tigeria. When Razor entered, she was already getting dressed in battle gear.

"Have you heard?" Razor asked.

"Yes," said Tigeria as she grabbed a picture of her mother that she kept hidden and kissed it.

"Do you ever miss mom?" she asked Razor.

"Now isn't the time," he grumbled as he left the room. Tigeria knew it bothered Razor not having their mother around. Razor went outside, where he and the troops waited for his sister. When she was finally dressed and ready, they began their ride towards Arias Kingdom.

"Are you all prepared?" Razor asked.

A resounding "YES!" exploded from the group of soldiers.

Up until then, Arias Kingdom had been quiet; however, around 6 p.m., there was a loud pounding on the ground from the horses accompanying Razor, Tigeria and his soldiers. The sound was startling, but most of the elders from Arias Kingdom knew what caused the noise. Alarmed, some of the parents started calling and going to search for their kids. Some of the young tigers began to scream and cry in fear. The elders and the townspeople became terrified as they could see Soldiers from Erland Kingdom coming out of the forest on horses—with Razor leading the troops.

Tylissa heard the noise as well. Before she went outside, she asked Clarence to go out the back door and head for the forest to find their daughter Tigris. Clarence asked why the back door, but Tylissa only shouted, "go Now!!" Tylissa exited her residence to deal with the arriving soldiers. Razor stopped the caravan as he slowly made his way to the center of the city.

"Come out!" Razor demanded of the townspeople, and the elder male tigers and male guards from Arias Kingdom stood in front of the women and children. Once there was an audience, Razor let the people of Arias Kingdom know, "I am here to collect the young girls, gold, silver and other jewels." The elders knew that this would happen because this was part of the peace treaty supposedly signed by King Shannon decades ago to save his kingdom from being slaughtered. The treaty stated that the Erland Kingdom can come and peacefully collect every three to five years. Elder John instructed some guards to go into the storage room to grab two trunks full of gold, silver and diamonds. The guards returned to the middle of the city cautiously, they presented the trunks to Razor.

He looked at the treasure and scoffed, "The payment is not enough! I need 20 daughters under the age of 16."

The parents of Arias Kingdom started screaming, panicking and holding on to their children. Frantically, Clarence continued her search for Tigris—but she was nowhere to be found. There was a little tigress that ran by Razor, and he attempted to grab her arm, but when Tylissa saw Razor reach to snatch her, she grabbed the little girl and pushed Razor's hand away. Razor shot his claws out to slice Tylissa, but she blocked his arms, then gave him a swift kick to his face knocking him down. This angered Razor, but before he could react, Tigeria jumped off her horse and tried to stab Tylissa with the two Sai swords she always carried. These swords were like a shorter version of a three-prong pitchfork with the middle prong longer than the outside prongs. Elder John threw Tylissa a sword, and she blocked Tigeria from stabbing her. Razor tried to stand back up, but Tylissa swiped his feet, causing him to fall back. Tigeria tried to kick Tylissa in the face, but Tylissa caught her right leg and pushed her to the ground as well. One of the soldiers from Erland Kingdom tried to dismount, but Tigeria put the sword to his neck and said, "Stay on your horse or die." The soldier quickly sat back on his horse.

Tigeria helped her brother Razor get to his feet. Then she reminded the people of the kingdom about the treaty signed by King Shannon. "And any objection to the treaty could result in war."

As Tigeria turned to walk away, Tylissa said, "Tell me, young lady, What's your mother's name?"

"What's it to you?" asked Tigeria. "She's dead anyway."

Tylissa approached Tigeria, and Tigeria was so scared—she reached for her staff, but before she could grab it, Tylissa caressed her face with her right hand and said, "I am sorry."

Tigeria became calm, never knowing the caressing touch of a woman. Razor stepped towards Tylissa, shooting out his claws, but she put her left hand on his face as well. His claws retracted, and he and his sister fell into a trance-like state for about 10 seconds as Tylissa stared into their eyes.

"Are you twins?" Tylissa asked them.

"Yes," replied Razor. A few seconds later, Razor commanded his sister and the troops to "mount and head out."

"Are you okay?" Tylissa asked the little girl. "Yes, I am. Thank you, my Queen." Tylissa smiled as she walked the girl to her mother. Tylissa saw a female tigress in the crowd who walked away, covering her head with a hood. She looked back at Tylissa, and they made eye contact for a brief second. Tylissa thought this lady looked familiar, but she was not sure, so she went to join Clarence to search for Tigris. While riding through the forest, Tigeria saw someone swinging on tree limbs being chased by sun bears and other animals out of the corner of her eye. Tigeria said to the soldiers, "Stop!" She concentrated on locating the commotion. Tigeria and Tigris made eye contact for a moment. Tigeria yelled, "Excuse me, are you okay?" Tigris disappeared into the forest, leaving Tigeria confused and worried. Razor said, "Let's go," and the caravan took off.

When Tylissa found Clarence, they both started calling Tigris' name. Some of the animals heard the call, and they let Tigris know by head movement and facial gestures that someone was calling for her. Tigris was able to interpret the animal's movements, sounds and facial gestures.

Tigris was in the river swimming with crocodiles she became friends with. Tigris was trying to hold her breath longer than the crocodile. She also imitated the moves that she saw the reptiles perform, like the death roll and leaping with half of their bodies coming out of the water. Tigris heard her parents calling her, and she said, "over here, mom and dad." Both parents ran over because she was in the river, and they knew it was full of crocodiles. Both parents yelled to Tigris, "Get out of the river!"

As they got closer to the river, Tigris went under. Both parents grabbed each other, and Clarence picked up a stick as he walked towards the river. Then suddenly, Tigris was shot out of the water by the snout of the crocodile. She performed two backflips landing perfectly in the water beside the crocodile. Tigris rubbed the crocodile snout, then gave it a kiss before she got out of the water.

Tylissa said to Tigris, "Are you okay?" she asked. "Yes, mother, those are my friends," as she winked at the crocodile before it went under. Clarence was quite amazed. "What is going on with the women in my life," he said as he chuckled then kissed his daughter. The family exited the forest to go home and have dinner. "Clarence asked Tylissa What happened?"

"I'll let you know later," she responded. After dinner and chores, both Clarence and Tylissa kissed their daughter goodnight. Clarence said to Tylissa, you look tired, and you should get some rest. Tylissa kissed Clarence and thanked him for understanding how she felt.

CHAPTER 9

Back in Erland Kingdom, Tigeria, Razor and the soldiers had just arrived. Tigeria and razor looked defeated. They both had confused looks on their faces because, for the first time, they both tasted defeat. "Let King Saber know what happened…and the troops and I will take the gold and silver inside," Razor said to Tigeria. She nodded yes. Razor waited until his sister was out of sight before giving some of the jewels to the soldiers that were in the claw gang. Razor and four of the claw gang members went to a room below in the basement to see what else they could steal from the bounty they took from Arias Kingdom. King Saber wanted to know what was taking so long, so he sent one treasurer Thaddeus to find Razor and bring back the jewels. Thaddeus has been a loyal servant to King Saber since he was kidnapped from his Kingdom twenty years ago. King Saber trusted Thaddeus like a son, so he made him the treasurer of Erland Kingdom. Thaddeus heard laughing and loud talking coming from the basement below, so he went to investigate. He was familiar with Razor's deep voice. Thaddeus opened the dungeon door, walked in on Razor and the troops, and asked, "What's going on here?"

"Counting gold and silver said Razor."

"That needs to be done in front of King Saber or myself," said Thaddeus. "The king MUST know of this betrayal."

"Wait!" said Razor, "let us meet in private…around the corner." The servant followed, and when they were out of public view, Razor had asked Thaddeus who he was dating. Thaddeus said that is none of your business! Razor grabbed Thaddeus' hand and kissed it. Thaddeus began to quiver, saying, "I like that a lot." Razor replied, "I thought you would." Razor pulled Thaddeus' head back, and he began to kiss his neck. Thaddeus shook and quivered even harder, begging him to keep going. When Thaddeus' eyes rolled back in his head due to the heated kiss, Razor unleashed his claws…followed by the sound of "slashing flesh" and a loud thump.

Some of the soldiers stepped around the corner and saw a body on the floor, and the head was about two feet away from the body. There was blood splattered on the walls and blood pouring on the floor from the neck of Thaddeus.

"Clean this up," he commanded the men. "And hide the body."

Quickly, they agreed.

In the meantime, Tigeria went to talk to her father, and when she arrived at his room, she knocked on the door. "Come in," said King Saber. Tigeria began to explain what went down in Arias Kingdom and King Saber asked, "Did you get jewels and tigresses?" Tigeria paused before replying, "We only got jewels because there was some resistance, and I couldn't bear to watch kids being taken from their parents." King Saber became furious and picked up Tigeria by her neck, lifting her off the floor. Her feet were dangling, and he shouted, "If you are a member of my family, you must obey orders or suffer consequences!" Afterward, he put her down and said, "Summon your brother!"

"Yes, my king…" she said, tears streaming down her face.

As she reached for the door, it was opened by Razor and some of the soldiers carrying the chest with gold and silver.

"What happened to Tigeria?" Razor asked King Saber.

"Never question me," he snapped in reply. After looking at the chest, "That's it?" he cried out. Tigeria looked and could tell some of the jewels were missing. She looked at Razor, and she gave him a look of shame.

"Can I be excused?" Tigeria asked.

"Go and think about the foolish mistake you made disobeying orders!" yelled King Saber. Tigeria walked away in shame, and as she did, she took a glance at Razor and saw that he had blood on himself and could see blood drops running down his arms. Razor asked Tigeria, "What's wrong?" but she just kept walking. Tigeria went to her room, and she cried a bit more, all the while holding a picture of her mom. Tigeria was still puzzled by the girl she saw in the forest. Tigeria overheard her brother Razor and King Saber stating that they needed more jewels and tigresses the next time they go. She put the pillow over her head, and she went to sleep.

CHAPTER 10

The next day Clarence was preparing to leave Arias Kingdom to go into the forest to see if he could locate the snakes that had eluded him before.

"Can I go?" Tigris asked.

"Don't you spend enough time there already?" Clarence replied. She smiled, and he said, "Sure, come on…but ask your mother first." Tigris yelled, "Mom!" who responded with the answer before she could ask, "Sure… you can go, but be very careful." Tigris packed a small lunch, and she and Clarence gave Tylissa a kiss goodbye.

"Watch over Tigris…"

"Shoot…she's the one who's going to take care of me!" Clarence jokes.

Clarence and Tigris headed for the forest. As Clarence walked a moderate pace, Tigris would take off in front in short bursts of speed, and Clarence would say, "Don't get too far ahead." Once Clarence and Tigris got to a certain location, Clarence let her know the specific snakes he was searching for. Tigris was excited because she has handled snakes before, and she has a relationship with all the forest creatures.

"Are you scared?" Clarence asked Tigris.

"Nope," she said, unbothered. "I have many snakes as friends."

"Well, these snakes are poisonous," cautioned Clarence.

"I know," she replied nonchalantly. Clarence looked at her, shook his head and said, "wow."

Clarence and Tigris walked further in the forest, and they came upon a log. "Let's lift this log," suggested Clarence—and when they did, they discovered a cobra, but not just any cobra. It was a spitting cobra. Clarence told Tigris to get back as he put on some goggles. He attempted to give her a pair of goggles as well, but she had already grabbed a leaf the size of an elephant ear to cover her eyes. Tigris began gently rubbing the cobra behind the head until it was in a trance. Tigris whispered something to the snake, and it came out of the trance.

"Pretty impressive," he said to her. Afterward, they sat down for a snack, which Tigris had prepared earlier. Clarence wanted to ask Tigris how she could hypnotize the snakes but decided against it and made small talk instead.

"Why aren't you eating your snacks?" he asked.

"I'm saving them for some of my animal friends."

"Okay," he replied, grabbing the gear. "Let's go."

"Aww…" she pleaded. "Can I stay a little while longer? I'll be careful and won't go into the water."

He paused, then reluctantly gave in. "Okay…you have one hour," he said, kissing her on the cheek.

"Thanks, Dad!" she said, then she jetted off with quickness of speed, jumping 10 feet into a tree to visit with her sun bear friends.

"I only have one hour to play," she hand signaled to her animal friends as she shared her snacks.

Tigris and the sun bears were having so much fun that they ended up in a part of the forest that was forbidden for tigers from Arias Kingdom to enter. Tigris motioned to her animal friends, "Let's turn around." Instead, one of the sun bears pointed towards the river, and they saw a horse alone, and it had clothes piled up next to it. Tigris and the sun bears were concerned, so they jumped down and approached quietly. As they got closer to the river, a beautiful tigress appeared out the river as she pulled her hair back with the water running down her body, and her womanly breasts were visible. Tigris covered the male sun bear's eyes, and the female sun bear laughed. The commotion caught Tigeria's attention. She looked over and saw them, which created a chuckle.

"Come into the river," she commanded.

Tigris was shocked because the lady was so beautiful. "Come on…I promise not to bite you. My name is Tigeria from Erland Kingdom, and your name is?"

"I am Tigris from Arias Kingdom…" she mumbled, confused by a tigress similar to herself.

"Does my nudity bother you?"

"No…" Tigris quickly replied, but her flushed cheeks and shy expression revealed her true embarrassment.

Tigris motioned for the sun bears to return to the trees. They followed her command but remained close. Tigris headed for the river, and she put her sack down and went in with a beautiful dive that barely made a splash. The two lady tigresses shook hands and started to play in the river, going under and throwing water at each other and chatting together.

"Are you hungry?" Tigeria asked Tigris.

"Yes," said Tigris.

"Let's get out and have a snack," suggested Tigeria, pointing to the other side of the river.

Tigris was hesitant because she knew it could be trouble to follow Tigeria to the other side where she was heading, but curiosity got the best of her. Tigeria climbed out of the water, and one of the male chimps was staring at her nakedness; his eyes rolled back in his head, and he collapsed on a limb while the other chimps giggled. Tigris was also staring at Tigeria's beautiful body. Tigeria looked back and saw Tigris staring…and Tigris turned her head real fast, making Tigeria smirk. Tigeria put on clothes and offered Tigris a towel as she could see that Tigris' nipples were hard and poking out.

"Are you cold?" she asked Tigris.

"Just a little…" she responded shyly.

Tigeria laid out a blanket, and she had some fruit and nuts, and the two began to snack and talk about things they like to do.

"Hey! Were you in the forest yesterday and with those same chimps?"

"Yes…that was me."

"We made eye contact for a brief moment," said Tigeria.

"Oh yeah…I remember," said Tigris. They smiled and laughed. After a short while, the sun bears signaled to Tigris that she had to leave, and Tigeria said, "Oh, you can communicate with them?"

"Yes," said Tigris. "I have to go," said Tigris. Tigeria gestured for the sun bears to come down. They all looked at Tigris for approval, and she gestured it was ok to come down. Tigris was amazed because she thought she was the only one that could communicate with wild animals.

"I've been coming to the forest for years learning about animals and their behaviors," explained Tigeria. When the sun bears came across the river, Tigeria offered them some nuts. After about ten minutes, Tigris said, "Let's go, guys!"

The chimp who was most fascinated with Tigris couldn't stop staring at Tigeria, so she swooped down, picked him up and kissed him on the cheek. Suddenly, his body went limp, and the other chimps giggled once more. Tigris laughed and thanked Tigeria for the snacks and conversation, and she turned to walk away when Tigeria asked, "Do you want to meet here tomorrow again?"

"Yes," responded Tigris feeling warm and fuzzy inside.

Suddenly, Tigeria grabbed Tigris and kissed her on the cheek. Tigris froze because she had never felt a feeling like she just experienced.

"Are you okay?" Tigeria asked Tigris.

"Oh yes…" Tigris responded, her nipples growing slowly.

"Oh," said Tigeria… "It must be *cold* out here." Tigris blushed and quickly covered her breasts with her arms.

CHAPTER 11

Razor had been thinking about the question his sister asked him as he and Tigeria walked down the hall. "Yes," he said to Tigeria. "I think about mother, and I wonder how things would have been with her in our lives. Would we be different if she were around?"

"Yes…I believe things would be different."

"I have this crazy feeling that she's still alive." They exchange looks at each other before getting to the dinner table to eat. King Saber rarely talks to his kids, but that night he asked them how their day was, and Tigeria said, "I had a nice relaxing day by the river," still thinking about Tigris.

"My day went well, but I was a little depressed and sad," said Razor.

"What happened?" King Saber asked. Tigeria looked at her brother and quietly whispered, "no, brother." Razor refused to listen to Tigeria, and instead, he asked, "Dad…what was our mother's name?"

All the guests stopped eating, and King Saber gripped his fork so hard it bent. One of the elders looked at King Saber, and he nodded. The elder guest asked all the other guests at the table to excuse themselves—leaving only King Saber, Razor and Tigeria. Tigeria gripped her brother's hand to support him. Although upset because he told the kids to never ask that question, King Saber proceeded to answer. And though King Saber was visibly upset, he said, "Queen Venus." He continued, "Your mother was from Siberia, like me, and she fought many battles with me. Eventually, we became the King and Queen of the Erland Kingdom.

Tigeria and Razor looked at each other in astonishment, "Our mother was a warrior?" they both asked.

"One of the best," confirmed King Saber.

Tigeria began to cry as she asked her father what happened. King Saber answered by saying, "one day she went to the river and never came back. All the tigers from Erland Kingdom and I searched for her…even asking the leader of Arias Kingdom to send troops to help. When my troops found her a week later, she was a different color from being in the water. It was obvious that she had drowned

His children were speechless. "I believe she was killed by a leader from Arias Kingdom who goes by the name of Tylissa…"

"I'm sorry, kids," he said. "I didn't want to tell you all of this because I know how painful it is." Razor and Tigeria both began to cry. Razor shot out his claws and scratched the table. King Saber asked, "My son, are you okay?"

"There was a lady," Razor reflected, "There was a lady, but I wasn't sure if she was a leader…she stopped me from grabbing tigress, performing a move I'd never seen, and managing to kick me in the face. Dad, she was so fast I couldn't land a hit."

King Saber's eyes widened as he knew there was only one tigress capable of moving like that—but his troops assured him that they had killed her in the forest. King Saber asked Razor and Tigeria to leave, and Tigeria thanked him as she held her brother, and they left the room. After they left, King Saber summoned his trusted general, whom everyone referred to as "General Thiger."

General Thiger, along with two other tigers, orchestrated the attempted murder of Tylissa. King Saber asked General Thiger, "Do you remember years ago when we assassinated Tylissa?"

"Yes…I remember," replied General Thiger.

"Are you sure she was murdered?" asked King Saber.

"Yes," said General Thiger. "You sent your two best warriors." But King Saber knew that wasn't enough for Tylissa and the skills she has.

"Did you get proof?" King Saber asked.

"No, my king…" said General Thiger.

"Then how do you know she's dead?"

General Thiger knew what would happen if he accidentally lied to King Saber. The general started to sweat, and his voice lowered,

"My assassins said they clawed her pretty good, and they're sure she bled out." King Saber pulled out his sword and slashed the floor, and put the sword up to the General's face, speaking under clenched teeth, "You better make sure she's dead," as he sliced the general's chin with the tip of his sword. The next morning Tigeria packed a bag and headed for the river to meet Tigris. Apart from thoughts of her mother, she could not get Tigris off her mind as she smiled, looking in the mirror. Tigeria loaded a sack of goods, placed them on the horse, and took off for the river. King Saber went to Razor's room, and the king walked in.

"What are you doing, Razor?" asked the king.

"Just thinking about mother and what it would be like to have one."

"I am so sorry," said King Saber. "Please…follow me, son."

Razor got up and followed his father. King Saber led Razor to the "strategic room," which Razor had never seen. The room was filled with elders and military personnel. Razor sat at the round table next to his father. General Thiger stood up and addressed the group.

"Overnight…I sent out two assassins, and they were able to collect valuable data," said General Thiger. "They were able to confirm that Tylissa is still alive."

"How do you know this?" asked King Saber. The assassins were able to capture a guard from Arias Kingdom, and they tortured him until he gave them the answers they sought."

King Saber grimaced with anger and screamed out, "I thought she was dead!!!!"

"I'm sorry, King," said General Thiger with deep regret on his face.

King Saber gave him a deadly stare and said, "I am contemplating if I should kill you *now* or later..." General Thiger sat back in his chair with a defeated look on his face. "A war is coming!" shouted King Saber, throwing intel papers in the air. King Saber demanded everyone present to keep his thoughts in this room, and he whispered in Razor's ear not to mention anything to his sister, Tigeria.

Tigeria met with Tigris at the same spot. Tigris and Tigeria embraced in a hug, and Tigris feeling very shy, kissed Tigeria on the cheek, and the two held hands and prepared lunch on the blanket Tigeria laid out on the ground. Tigeria prepared some deer and vegetables on a plate, and the two ate a light lunch. Tigeria asked Tigris, "Have you ever been in a relationship?"

"What is a relationship?" Tigris asked.

"You know..." said Tigeria, "When two people are in love, they consider themselves in a relationship, for example, boyfriend/girlfriend, boyfriend/boyfriend, or in our case, girlfriend/girlfriend..." and she kissed Tigris on the lips. The two locked lips for about twenty seconds, then Tigris pulled back, and Tigeria asked Tigris, "What's wrong?"

"The tongue touching made me feel funny..." said Tigris.

Tigeria chuckled. "Hopefully, it was a good funny feeling."

"Oh, it was..." Tigris responded shyly.

The two held hands and walked around the forest for a little while. While walking, Tigeria picked up a flower. "Will you be my girlfriend?" Tigeria asked Tigris. "Yes," she said while giggling. The two tigresses went back to Tigeria's horse, and Tigris helped her load things up and the two embraced in a hug and a deep kiss. Tigris kissed Tigeria on the neck, and Tigeria's eyes rolled back into her head.

"Oh my god! Who taught you that?" asked Tigeria.

"My father does it to my mother," said Tigris. "Was I wrong to do that?" she asked nervously.

"No… it felt incredibly good in that spot. By the way…my father is King Saber, and I don't have a mother," said Tigeria. "I just wanted to let you know that."

"Oh…okay. Well, my father is Clarence, and my mother's name is Tylissa."

"Tylissa…?" stammered Tigeria.

"Yes…Tylissa," said Tigris.

"Is your mom a leader in Arias Kingdom?"

"I'm not sure," said Tigris, "but people listen to her."

Tigeria paused for a moment to reflect upon one big problem: she was in love with the daughter of her father's enemy. But she did not articulate the thought. She simply kissed Tigris goodbye, and the two made plans to meet again later in the week.

CHAPTER 12

Tylissa was at home preparing dinner, and her thoughts were consumed with Razor and Tigeria and how awful it was that they didn't know their mother. While cooking, she dropped some pots and pans. Clarence asked, "Are you okay?" Clarence knew that Tylissa was acting differently from her usual self—losing focus and spacing off when he tried to talk to her. Tylissa first apologized to Clarence for yelling at him when the soldiers showed up. Clarence mentioned that he understood the importance of finding Tigris then he hugged and kissed her. Tylissa stated that she was worried about the safety of the Kingdom and worried about the twins from Erland Kingdom. Clarence said, "Help me understand something about this treaty…"

"Okay," Tylissa agreed to tell Clarence. She let Clarence know that soldiers could come every three to five years to collect young female tigers and all types of jewels as part of a peace treaty.

"So, troops from Erland Kingdom can just come and get jewels and tigresses anytime they want?"

"Unfortunately, yes…" she said, "but *only* with permission from King Saber. My father, King Shannon, signed this treaty supposedly while on his deathbed. I was too young to remember…and at that time, my only concern was the health of my father." Tylissa explained that her parents King Shannon and Queen Mary, were weak from being poisoned, and there weren't many fighters, "so to save the kingdom from being slaughtered, he signed this treaty, but there were no witnesses from Arias Kingdom who saw this."

"That sounds pretty sketchy to me," remarked Clarence.

"I agree, but there is no way to find out because the guards who poisoned my parents were also found dead." Tylissa further explained to Clarence that the guards pretended to defect from Erland Kingdom and pledge their loyalty to my father, King Shannon, but they had devious intentions the whole time. Clarence asked Tylissa what else was bothering her?

Tylissa said, "a woman was in the crowd when the Soldiers from Erland Kingdom came to get jewels and tigresses, but I don't know who this woman was."

"Give it time…you will eventually run into her," Clarence said.

Tigris came into the house just in time for dinner, and Clarence said, "wash your hands."

"I will," she said. At the dinner table, Tylissa and Clarence looked at Tigris, and they both observed her giddy nature. "Why are you smiling and giggling?"

"Oh…I'm sorry…" she said, embarrassed they had noticed.

"Well…who is that someone, or what is that something responsible for your new smile?"

"Tigris…so are you going to tell us *his* name?" Clarence asked.

And Tigris spit out some of the salad she was eating and said, "dad stop it."

"Yes, tell us his name," said Tylissa.

"Mom, dad…why are you asking me that?"

"We've been paying close attention to your appearance and choice of clothes." Tigris went silent as she blushed, and her face turned red.

"I don't have a boyfriend," she insisted.

"Okay…well…your friend who he is," said Clarence.

"It's not he…but a *she*," said Tigris.

"This is great!" said her mother, "because you rarely have female friends."

"She's not my friend…she's my girlfriend."

Clarence stopped eating and looked at Tylissa, who had a blank stare on her face. A quiet, hushed silence overcame the dinner table, and all three kept eating after a minute of awkward silence. After dinner, Clarence asked Tigris to clean the plates and wash the dishes, and Tigris replied, "yes, father." Clarence and Tylissa sat at the table. "What do you think about her having a girlfriend?" Tylissa responded, "I'm not sure."

"Well, if it was a boyfriend, I would handle it, but since it's a girl…good luck," he said with a smile.

"Hey! Not fair!"

Clarence laughed and excused himself. While Tigris was cleaning dishes, Tylissa joined, putting her hand on her daughter's shoulder. Tylissa took a different approach as most parents would when finding that their child has an interest in the same sex.

"So…who's this girl that my daughter thinks she's in love with?" Tigris went on to explain that she thought Tigeria was the most beautiful girl she ever met.

"Is that right?" Tylissa asked.

Tigris explained that Tigeria had physical features that she hadn't seen on any tigress in Arias Kingdom.

"How long have you two been seeing each other?"

"I only met her twice…but one time was all that was needed."

"Okay," said Tylissa with a smile.

Tylissa and Tigris walked to the sitting area, and Tylissa let Tigris know that a relationship like that has never been seen around Tigelandia and that such a relationship was forbidden.

"Explain forbidden?" asked Tigris.

"Well…" said her mother, "the people of the kingdom do not approve of same-sex relationships…and they seek to remove those involved in such a relationship, abolishing them from the kingdom forever."

Tigris became upset, and she started to cry; she got up quickly and headed for her room.

"Tigris! Come back!" pleaded Tylissa, but Tigris continued to her room, where she closed and locked the door. Tigris sat on her bed with her head on her knees. Clarence overheard part of the conversation, and he met Tylissa in the hallway.

"Do you need some help?" he asked his Tylissa.

"I'll handle it," she replied. Tylissa knocked several times, and eventually, Tigris unlocked the door. Tylissa entered the room and sat on the bed next to her daughter.

"Baby, I am sorry," said Tylissa. "I can see that you really care for this girl, but our kingdom has rules, and without rules, we have no structure."

Tigris' crying eased, and she said, "What a dumb rule!"

"I agree with you, daughter. You can visit your girlfriend one more time...but only to explain why you can't be with her."

"It isn't fair, mom!"

"Sometimes...life isn't fair," said Tylissa, giving Tigris a hug.

"Okay, mom...I know what must be done. I'll speak to my girlfriend."

"By the way...where does she live?" Tylissa asked. Tigris knew that the two kingdoms were at war, so she told her mom a lie, "Oh...she's from a small village near Tigelandia."

"Okay," Tylissa said. "What's her name?"

"Mom…I don't want to say it."

"Ok, my love…"

Tylissa went back to kiss Tigris on the cheek, and Clarence came into the room and kissed his daughter on the cheek as well, and both parents said goodnight. The next day Tylissa took a walk through the kingdom, looking for the lady she had seen at the scuffle. Tylissa stopped a couple of people, giving them a brief description of the woman, but none of the tigers recognized the description. After about an hour of walking and questioning the people of her kingdom, Tylissa headed back home when she heard a voice say, "Hello Tylissa, I heard you were looking for me."

Tylissa finally came face to face with the lady she had etched in her head for the past week. Tylissa reached out her hand to greet the tigress, and the tigress shook her hand, saying, "it's nice to meet you again."

"Please forgive me, but I don't remember our first encounter."

"Please walk with me," said the tigress, and the two walked towards the forest.

"We met about eighteen years ago when you pulled me out of the river," said the tigress.

Tylissa turned towards the lady, screaming, "Yes! Yes! I remember…but I don't remember your name because I had forgotten about that incident." Tylissa grabbed the tigress by the shoulders and said, "Look at you…your wounds are all healed up, and you are looking stronger and healthier."

"I owe it all to you, and I always wanted to thank you, but after all these years, I never had the courage…but once I saw you stand up to those soldiers from Erland Kingdom, I gained the confidence to talk to you." Tylissa said, "if I had had the chance to do it all over I would." The tigress said, "eighteen years ago I told you my name was Tyglina…"

Tylissa said, "that sounds familiar." The tigress apologized to Tylissa, and Tylissa asked, "Why are you apologizing?"

"My name isn't Tyglina. I am Queen Venus, wife of King Saber, and mother of the twins you encountered the other day."

Tylissa stood there in shock and awe as she put her hand on each side of the queen's face and stared into her eyes.

Queen Venus is the wife of King Saber and the mother of the twins, Tigeria and Razor. Queen Venus is six feet two inches tall with a blonde mane, and her eyes are blue, orange and white like the planet Venus. This is how she got the name Queen Venus. She has a slim build and is originally from Cambodia.

She met King Saber in the Erland Kingdom when she was taken there to fight for money and jewels. Queen Venus is a great fighter who was handpicked by the elders to fight for the Erland kingdom. The kingdom lacked fighters, so they sent out requests to pay skilled fighters to fight for The Kingdom. In return, fighters were given a place to live and were paid in money and gold. Everyone in Erland Kingdom believed that Queen Venus was dead. She rarely agreed with King Saber, and all the people of Erland Kingdom loved her more than the King. Many believed this was the reason he tried to kill her.

"Yes…I can see the eyes and the resemblance in your face," said Tylissa. "I knew there was a reason I couldn't stop thinking about the incident or get the thought of the twins out of my head."

Tylissa grabbed Queen Venus's hand and said, "Walk with me…" and the Queen covered back up and followed Tylissa to her residence.

CHAPTER 13

Tigeria awakened to the sounds of swords hitting each other. She was familiar with that sound when Soldiers were outside training, but she found it odd that it was so early in the morning. She also noted that it was more than a couple of Soldiers—it was the whole military conducting fighting drills and exercising. Tigeria put on her gear, grabbed her staff and went to join the training exercises. When she reached the training, she saw her brother, Razor, working on his defenses, but prior to her arrival, Razor had already told the men, "Remember…it's only training. Don't mention the battle ahead."

"Brother, you didn't tell me about the training," said Tigeria.

"I didn't want to wake you," confessed Razor. "And besides…it's more like play."

"This looks like more than training," she replied, "but oh well…let us play."

Tigeria performed a backflip, slashed her staff downwards towards Razor but he shot out his claws, crossing his arms and blocking Tigeria's staff. "Nice job, brother," said Tigeria as she performed a handstand, dropping the staff between her legs and confusing Razor. She pulled out a small sword pressing it against his stomach, "I gotcha." Razor looked down and shook his head. A deep voice said, "You are weak and need to focus!" It was his father, King Saber. Razor shook his head in disappointment, and Tigeria said, "Don't get upset…just focus." Razor nodded yes. Razor and his sister trained for about thirty more minutes, then they both headed inside.

"Father never comes to training," Tigeria said to Razor. "Isn't that a little strange?"

"Let it go," he said, as he rubbed his shoulder against hers playfully. Later that night, after dinner, Tigeria asked Razor to step outside with her. The two walked away from the kingdom towards the forest.

"I have something to tell you, brother."

"What is it?"

"I think I'm in love," Tigeria confessed.

"Really?" asked Razor surprised. "What's his name?"

"I'm not going to tell you that."

"Well, where is he from?"

"A small village, not far from Erland Kingdom."

"Congratulations!" said Razor, "and yes, I will keep it a secret." Razor and Tigeria knew King Saber would never approve of her being with someone outside of the kingdom. Tigeria hugged her brother, and they headed back home. Tigeria went to her room thinking about Tigris, grabbed her pillow tight and fell asleep.

The next day Tigeria lay in bed thinking about Tigris. The very thought made her smile and have warm feelings through her body as she began caressing her breasts. Suddenly, there was a commotion outside. Tigeria walked over to her window, and she could see a gathering of tigers consisting of the kingdom elders, soldiers and civilians who lived in Erland Kingdom. Tigeria quickly put on some clothes and ran downstairs. Tigeria ran into Razor and asked, "What's going on?"

"Father is about to hand down punishment to General Thiger and two assassins that worked for General Thiger.

"What did the General and those two tigers do?" she asked. Razor didn't want Tigeria to know the truth about their failure to kill Tylissa, so instead, he said, "That's all you need to know right now."

The troops brought the General and the two tigers to the center of the circle, and all three Tigers were gagged, blindfolded and their hands tied behind their backs. King Saber began speaking and the crowd fell silent because no one else could speak when King Saber was speaking.

King Saber declared, "Traitors to the kingdom aren't allowed!"

General Thiger started to shake his head, trying to scream because he did not want his family to think he was a traitor, but they couldn't hear or understand him.

"General Thiger and the two corrupt assassins gave secrets plans to key leaders from Arias Kingdom!" declared King Saber. The crowd gasped and shouted, "Trader! Trader! Trader!" Tigeria knew General Thiger and his family, and she could not believe this. King Saber shouted, "This kind of behavior isn't to be tolerated in this kingdom!" The three tigers were standing next to each other, and two of them had tears rolling down their face. King Saber continued, "This crime is punishable by death!" He reached for his sword, the largest in all Tigelandia, and Tigeria knew what came next, so she went to cover the eyes of General Thiger's kids and said to his wife, "Please don't look!" King Saber placed his sword on the shoulder of one of the three Tigers so he could get leverage, and in one stroke, beheaded all the tigers with one swing of his massive sword. Tigeria grabbed the general kid's as General Thiger's wife fell to the ground in pain and agony. Tigeria rushed the kids inside the Kingdom. She hated violence and felt horrible for General Thiger's family. Razor saw the disgust on Tigeria's face, and he went to console her.

"Was this necessary?" Tigeria blurted while comforting the kids.

"I know it's bad, but we must follow the laws set in place by our King," said Razor.

"This wasn't fair! Father could've done this privately and not make it a public event." Razor said he was sorry to Tigeria as she turned and apologized to the children, who continued to cry, asking, "What happened to our father?"

The wife of General Thiger came over to Tigeria and thanked her for helping, and she left with the kids, and they headed home.

"Is she going to be ok?"

"Yes…" she said, "I will see you at dinner."

Later that night, Razor and Tigeria were sitting at the dinner table with King Saber.

"Father, why did you have a public execution?"

"The purpose…" he said in a booming voice, "to cause fear in everyone in Erland Kingdom and let them know that disobeying the king is unacceptable."

Tigeria winced.

"How did you feel about it?"

"It didn't bother me at all…" she lied, holding in her truth. Razor knew it was a lie as he felt sympathy for his sister.

CHAPTER 14

Tylissa and Queen Venus eventually arrived at Tylissa's residence.

"Have a seat," Tylissa said.

"Thank you…please call me Venus."

"How did you keep her identity a secret for so many years?"

"I had to…for the sake of my twins, Tigeria and Razor. I isolated myself and refused to get involved in any kind of personal relationship because I was afraid someone would recognize me. I even wore a mask on some occasions."

"Do you miss your kids?" Tylissa asked.

"Every second," Queen Venus confirmed. "I returned to the forest many times to spy on my children…but was never able to get close enough."

"How did you end up in the river half dead?" Tylissa asked Queen Venus.

"King Saber and I got into an argument about Arias Kingdom."

"Please explain," said Tylissa.

"I overheard King Saber say he planned to execute you and all the Tigers in Arias Kingdom. The next day, I confronted King Saber and asked him not to do this. King Saber was worried about you building an army and someday coming to eliminate him. I told King Saber not to go through with this, but his mind was made up, and there wasn't anything I could do to stop him. So, I pretended that the twins and I were terribly ill so that King Saber could stay close. This caused the King to put his plans of attacking your Kingdom on hold."

"I see…" said Tylissa with a heavy heart but also grateful.

"After the twins were born…they became my main focus, and I no longer wanted to be a warrior or part of any more wars." Tylissa handed Queen Venus some hot tea and sat beside her.

"Your father, King Shannon, was a strong leader and a great warrior who King Saber has always envied…" said Queen Venus. Tylissa grabbed her hand and thanked her.

"The main reason King Saber tried to eliminate me was that he feared I would tell the truth about the treaty," said Queen Venus.

"What about the treaty?" asked Tylissa. "Please tell me!"

"Your father never signed the treaty," confessed Queen Venus. Tylissa became enraged as she stood up, "What!!! What are you telling me?"

"Your father was invited to Erland Kingdom to sign a peace treaty. King Saber invited King Shannon and his loyal members from his personal military to have wine, dinner and discuss a peace treaty. The wine was laced with poison, but it didn't take effect until King Shannon and his military members almost reached Arias Kingdom. King Shannon became extremely sick and nearly died, but two of his high-ranking generals weren't so lucky because they died from the poisoning within an hour. Tylissa's face was frozen in shock. "King Shannon eventually returned to health, but it did last long because King Saber found out that the poison wasn't effective and that's when King Saber had two troops pretend to defect, and they had orders to kill the King and his wife, Queen Mary. There was no treaty. Everything was fabricated…all a lie."

In outrage, Tylissa punched the wall. "All those jewels and young tigresses over all the years…" and she began to weep.

"I was on an expedition during that time and had returned home, only to hear about my parents."

I had threatened to tell you and the people of your kingdom," Queen Venus said. "King Saber became upset. Later in the day, he asked me to go for a ride in the forest with him and his guards. Not thinking, I went. At the river's edge, we dismounted. King Saber embraced me, telling me how much he loved me…but said the kingdom comes before me! I knew I was in imminent danger, so I tried to pull away…but King Saber was stronger."

"Oh my God!" said Tylissa.

"I eventually got away, turned around and ran into one of the guards standing there holding a sword. The weapon went through my abdomen. I screamed out in pain and turned to look at King Saber for help…but he just stood there with his hands behind his back as he calmly told his guards to finish me. Tylissa was in utter disbelief.

"One Tiger thrust his sword deeper, and another guard stabbed me in the back. I fell to the ground in pain and agony and pretended to play dead. Eventually, I was thrown into the river by King Saber."

"This isn't fair!" said Tylissa. "King Saber robbed the twins of a life with their mom."

Meanwhile, Clarence and Tigris sat on the back porch. Tigris asked her father what he thought about the relationship with her and another female. Clarence said, "not uncommon, but nothing about being in this place has surprised me." He hugged Tigris. "I support you 100% no matter who you love. My job is to protect you from those who wish to cause harm to you and your mother. Young people go through ups and downs in relationships, and being hurt is a part of dating."

"Mom told me to break it off," said Tigris.

"Listen to your mother because she knows more about this place than I do."

Clarence and Tigris walked into the living quarters, and Clarence could see that Tylissa was crying and upset. Clarence asked, "What's wrong?"

"I just found out how my parents were murdered…" said Tylissa.

"How mommy?" said Tigris.

"Go play Tigris. I need to talk to your dad...adult business."

Tigris went to her room, grabbed a bag and filled it with treats as she was going to go to the forest to play with her friends. Tigris kissed both her father and mother on the cheek and headed for the door, but before she could close the door, Tylissa said, "Don't forget what I mentioned to you about your special friend."

"Yes, mom," said Tigris.

Tylissa introduced Clarence to Queen Venus and let him know she was once the Queen of Erland Kingdom and King Saber's wife. Clarence put his hands up, not really knowing who the people behind the names were.

"Sit down," she asked Clarence.

Tylissa went on to explain to Clarence how her parents were murdered, and she vowed vengeance. Tylissa said, "As long as I'm alive, the treaty isn't to be upheld. All the people of the kingdom should know this.

"Wouldn't this start a war?" asked Clarence.

Tylissa said, "I am ready for war."

Clarence and Queen Venus looked at each other as they could see the anger in Tylissa's eyes.

"I need to speak with King Saber."

"That would be suicide."

"Why is that?"

"King Saber believes that we are both dead."

"What?" asked Tylissa.

Queen Venus said, "one of my sources told me that King Saber wanted you killed, and that little incident where you were injured was a planned attack to kill you." Clarence's jaw dropped as he said, "Wait! That's the day we met!"

"Yes!" said Tylissa, with anger and confusion plastered on her face.

CHAPTER 15

It was Saturday evening, and King Saber was sitting at the kitchen table eating dinner with Razor. King Saber said, "Razor, one of the ways to win a battle is the element of surprise."

"Yes, father," replied Razor. "I will remember that."

"This is the reason we are bringing the battle to Arias Kingdom in the morning."

"What!?!" exclaimed Razor, eyes widened.

"I just told you about the element of surprise."

Razor nodded, "Yes, father."

King Saber asked Razor, "Go tell the guards to prepare for battle tomorrow and ask the Generals to meet me in the kitchen."

"Yes, dad," said Razor.

"And don't mention anything to your sister," he warned.

"Yes, dad."

Razor exited quietly, walking through the kingdom, telling Generals to meet in the kitchen and letting the guards know about the battle tomorrow. And with that, some of the guards began preparing their battle equipment. King Saber spoke with the Generals in a soft tone as he told the Generals, "the plan is to attack Arias Kingdom when they least expect it." All the Generals approved of the plan, but in actuality, they had no choice but to agree. Meanwhile, Tigeria sat in her room thinking about Tigris, and she was happy that they were going to meet the next day. Tigeria was trying on different outfits to see which one made her look sexier. Tigeria was so excited that her bags were already packed for her date with Tigris. Tigeria had it in her mind that she was going for more than a kiss and a hug as she lay on the bed in the nude and prepared to go to sleep.

That next morning King Saber sat on his horse in the middle of the kingdom square in full battle gear and his five-foot sword polished and visible in his right hand. It was very intimidating for all to see a weapon so big, and everyone most certainly feared him. All the guards on horses positioned themselves in formation as King Saber asked the military to remain quiet as possible as the king dismounted and walked through the line of guards, telling the soldiers how brave they were. "Some of you may not return," he said with a solemn tone. The guards held their swords up and said quietly, "We are willing to die for the Erland Kingdom." King Saber nodded his head and said, "That's what I want to hear. Okay…dismount quietly." They obeyed and walked the horses in the forest.

Tigeria awakened with one thing on her mind—Tigris. She took a shower and dressed. Tigeria wore a short black dress that was barely above her knees. As Tigeria entered the kitchen, walking through the hallways, she could see that things were eerily quiet. Tigeria went to Razor's room and knocked on his door, but there was no answer. Tigeria asked one of the village elders, "Where is everyone?"

"The military is training," responded the elder.

Tigeria was a little upset that she wasn't invited, but she knew she would be happy as soon as she met Tigris. Tigeria went back to her room and grabbed her bags, then she loaded them on her horse.

Meanwhile, in Arias Kingdom, Tigris was collecting her usual snacks for her forest friends. After breakfast, Tigris told her parents that she was going to the forest.

"Again?" Clarence teased. Tigris smiled and kissed both of her parents on the cheek. Clarence looked at Tigris as she walked away and said to Tylissa, "What a great daughter we created." Tylissa smiled and said, "Yes...we did." Tigris made it to the forest, and her sun bears friends were waiting for her, so she jumped in the tree like she normally does. She shared the snacks amongst her forest friends. The sun bears signaled to Tigris that her friend was waiting on the other side of the river sitting on a blanket. Tigris was so excited and quickly headed in the direction of Tigeria. She dismounted with a backflip to show off, and Tigeria clapped her hands and said, "That was very impressive." Tigris and Tigeria embraced and looked back at the forest creatures who looked away as they locked lips and kissed for about ten seconds. Tigeria said to Tigris, "I couldn't wait to see you."

"I feel the same way," said Tigris.

They both sat down on the blanket and began to enjoy fruit and nuts. After small talk, Tigeria grabbed Tigris and pulled her closer, and said, "I'm in love with you." Tigris didn't really know what that meant but replied, "I feel the same way." They kissed as Tigeria laid Tigris down on the blanket and started kissing her neck and sliding her tongue up and down Tigris' neck. Tigris started to quiver as she began to shake with passion, crossing and uncrossing her legs. Tigeria grabbed Tigris' breast with both hands and licked Tigris' nipples with her tongue, causing goosebumps all over Tigris' body. Tigris asked, "What's happening to me?" Tigeria said, "It's very normal, and the goosebumps mean you love this. Tigris told Tigeria to continue.

It was Sunday afternoon, and most of the tigers in Arias Kingdom were in their homes, some preparing lunch and others sipping tea relaxing when they heard a familiar sound, but this time, the sound meant war. Some of the old fighters started to put on their battle gear while telling the younger tigers to get ready for war. Clarence heard the noise before Tylissa, and he asked, "Do you hear that?" Tylissa paused for a second before hearing the ground rumble. Tylissa grabbed Clarence by both shoulders, then handed him a sword and said, "Please listen to me! Go find Tigris and keep her in the forest."

"What's going on?" he asked.

"Just do what I said…right now!"

Clarence had never seen his wife afraid, so he knew she meant business. Tylissa went into her room, and she prepared for battle. Tylissa feared this day would come, but she did not think it was anytime soon. Tylissa was all geared up, and when she made it outside, there were already fights taking place, and she immediately joined in on the action. Tylissa was mowing down fighters from Erland Kingdom with no problems. But some of the town elders from Arias Kingdom weren't faring so well, and she tried to help them as much as possible. The first group of men King Saber sent out were his weakest fighters, and Tylissa and the fighters from Arias Kingdom eventually defeated them. After the dust settled, Tylissa made eye contact with King Saber for the first time. King Saber proclaimed in a very deep voice, "Tylissa, daughter of King Shannon!"

"King Saber, murderer and liar!" she shouted back, striking her sword to the ground, and said, "we will no longer honor that treaty."

King Saber's face became enraged. He shouted to his son, "You and the troops…attack!"

Razor shot out his claws and shouted, "Kill everyone…but leave HER for me," he said, pointing to Tylissa. By this time, Clarence had reached the forest, and he started calling Tigris' name. Clarence screamed as loud as he could, "Tigris…where are you?" Clarence ran deeper into the forest screaming, "Tigris…where are you?" One of the chimps screamed out in the direction of Tigris and Tigeria. The two tigresses let go of each other. Tigris looked at Tigeria and asked, "What's wrong?"

Clarence got closer. He screamed again, "Tigris!"

"Yes, father…" she answered.

Clarence came close to the river's edge and said, "Something is going on in the Kingdom. I need you here with me."

"What happened…" Tigris asked. "Where is mom?"

"Tigris, come here now!" Clarence demanded.

Tigris went to her father. Another sun bear came running, signaling to Tigris that there was a battle going on. Tigris asked, "a battle?" Tigeria asked the sun bears using sign language where? The sun bears looked at Tigris for approval. Tigris said it was okay and the sun bears signaled a battle was happening in Arias Kingdom. Tigeria packed her things and mounted her horse. Tigeria went to the other side of the river. She introduced herself to Clarence, and they briefly shook hands. Tigris screamed, "Oh no! What about mom?"

Clarence told Tigris, "Your mom said for you to stay here."

Tigris said, "No, I want to go and see my mother."

"We can get there faster by horse," said Tigeria.

There was nothing Clarence could do as Tigris climbed on the horse with Tigeria. Before Tigris left, she signaled to all the animals to help her father get back home. All the animals agreed with a nod of the head. Tigris yelled to her father as she rode, "the animals will help get you home."

Clarence said, "okay…please be safe."

Back at the battle, Razor mentioned to Tylissa that last time he wasn't ready, but now he was. He swung his arms down in a downward motion with his claws protruding from both hands, but Tylissa blocked him with a sword and said, "Let's play, young one." Razor became upset, and he started to swing his hands back and forth with all his attempts being blocked by Tylissa's sword. Tylissa could see that her fighters were losing to the younger, more agile tigers from Erland Kingdom, but she could not help as she had to deal with Razor. Tylissa didn't want to hurt Razor, so she kicked him then hit him with the handle of the sword. Then that familiar silhouette appeared like it did at the last scuffle, but this time, whoever it was pulled out a sword and started mowing down fighters from Erland Kingdom with no problem. This Tiger had a unique set of fighting skills not seen before. King Saber gave it a close look but didn't pay too much attention. At this time, King Saber asked two of the best fighting generals to dismount and fight. These were two of the best fighters from Erland Kingdom. The Generals were identical twin brothers from Northeast China. Their names were Lee and Li. The two brothers were skilled in martial arts and skilled at using traditional Chinese weapons. They became famous for being two of the best assassins around, boasting of a 100% kill rate. Lee went after the hooded figure while Li went after Tylissa, who was easily handling Razor. Tylissa knew who was behind the hood, but she was amazed to know that another tigress could match her fighting skills. The hooded figure went toe to toe with Lee—their swords clanking back and forth. It was a draw as no one could get the upper hand. While Tylissa had her sword locked with General Li, she was also fighting Razor—who went low, slashing her bottom leg deeply. She yelled out in pain. Tylissa resorted to fighting on one leg, hopping and bleeding profusely. Li noticed Tylissa was wounded, and he saw his chance to take advantage of her—so he rushed her with his sword held high, gripping the handle with two hands. Tylissa fell to the ground. General Li put his all into trying to stab through her chest, but as soon as he got close with the sword, Tylissa rolled to the right and stabbed Li through his right leg, causing him to fall to the ground face forward. When General Li hit the ground, Tylissa took her sword and stabbed General Li through his back, piercing his heart and killing him instantly. The cut in Tylissa's leg was bleeding badly. She tried to cover it with her hand. Razor saw his opportunity to end Tylissa's life, so he ran towards her, claws extended, but the hooded figure saw what was happening. The hooded fighter went around Lee's back, jumped up, wrapped both legs around his neck, and flipped backward, causing the general to flip as well, landing on his chest. Then the hooded fighter stuck the sword right through Lee's throat, killing him. King Saber only knew one person that could do a move like this, so he jumped off his horse, clearly frustrated, wondering who this person was as he drew his five-foot sword from his back.

Tigeria and Tigris made good time on the horse, and they were about to reach the clearing of the forest when Tigeria told Tigris to dismount, and they stood behind the tree. Tigeria could see her brother and her father, King Saber, and she became upset that they were attacking and killing the people of Arias Kingdom. Tigris asked Tigeria what was going on, and Tigeria explained that her kingdom was attacking hers. Tigris began to cry and asked, "Why would you do that?"

Tigeria told Tigris, "I'm sorry. I had no idea this was happening." Tylissa laid on the ground in a vulnerable position, and Razor was about to deliver the death blow when a voice called out to Razor? "Is that my son, Razor?" He stood up, and with a confused look on his face as the fighter took off the hood, it was Queen Venus.

"It's me, Razor…your mother."

"Nooo! It's not possible; it can't be!" said King Saber. Razor, looking surprised with his mouth open, said, "Mom?"

"Yes," she replied, rubbing his face. Razor began to cry but remained confused.

Tigeria came out of the forest and shouted, "Mom!" with tears in her eyes.

"My princess!" shouted Queen Venus, running towards her daughter. King Saber stood with his mouth open, disgusted and not knowing what to do. The two twins hugged their mom tightly.

"Father said you were dead," confessed the twins

Queen Venus told the twins it was their father who tried to kill her, and the kids looked at their father with disgust. Razor became so upset he went after his father but was knocked away by King Saber's sword. Tigeria pulled out her staff and angrily ran towards her father, trying to stab him, but she too was knocked aside. King Saber advanced towards Tylissa, declaring, "I will handle this myself!" as he pulled his big sword from his back. A noise came out of the forest. All anyone could see was a blurred shadow moving so quickly they couldn't identify it until it got closer. All the tigers walk upright, so everyone stopped what they were doing because they were witnessing a tiger run on all four legs. This scared a lot of tigers who never saw this. As King Saber attempted to swing his sword, Tigris pounced twenty feet in the air, and when she was coming down, she landed a kick to King Saber's face knocking him down and causing him to lose his sword. Tigris then circled around King Saber on all four legs like a beast circling its prey before attacking. King Saber yelled; how can you possess the forbidden stance?" King Saber mentioned only King Shannon could do this!

No one had ever seen King Saber look defeated as he laid on the ground in shock. King Saber regained his balance and stood up and faced everyone. Queen Venus had a sword to his throat, Razor had his claws to his head, and Tigeria had her staff pressed against his chest where his heart was.

Queen Venus said, "Leave now or die."

King Saber directed his men to get on their horse and head for the forest. As King Saber went to grab his sword, Queen Venus said, "leave it."

"What!?" King Saber protested.

"Leave it or die next to it…" commanded Queen Venus.

King Saber got on his horse, joining his men as they headed for the forest. Tigris caressed her mother's face, and Tylissa told Tigris not to cry, but Tigris couldn't stop the tears from flowing. Tigris asked her mom, "How can I stop your bleeding?"

"Baby, it's too late."

"No…please don't say that!" Tigris shouted.

At this time, Clarence cleared the forest and saw Tylissa on the ground. Clarence ran as fast as he could, eventually making it to Tylissa's side.

"What happened?" he asked in a panic.

"Wound from the battle," she said weakly.

Clarence looked at the wound and knew that there was nothing he could do to stop the bleeding. The sword had punctured an artery. Tylissa said, "Clarence, please promise me you will take care of our daughter."

Clarence held Tylissa's hand and said, "I will, but please don't die."

Tylissa called to Tigeria, "Come here, young lady. You're the beautiful girl that my daughter was talking about?"

"Yes…it's me…" Tigeria said. Tylissa touched her face causing Tigeria to cry even harder.

"Please take care of my daughter," said Tylissa to Tigeria.

"I promise I will," said Tigeria.

"My princess, said Tylissa to her daughter, "promise me you will take care of your father."

"Yes, mother…but PLEASE don't go!" Tigris begged.

"Honey, it will be alright…." promised Tylissa.

"No, mom! Please…" Tigris begged.

"Never forget that you are a very special person…" Clarence kissed his wife, and so did Tigris as she wept, "Please don't die." Queen Venus took off her cloak and covered Tylissa's body.

~ The End

ABOUT THE AUTHOR

Clarence Copeland Jr. is the author of Tigris. A Behavioral Health Technician professional by day, novelist by night, he received his bachelor of Science in Health, Physical Education and Recreation from Oklahoma Panhandle State University and his Masters Degree in Addiction Counseling from Grand Canyon University. A father of four, three sons and one daughter, he was born in Miami Florida, but now resides in Phoenix. He is a lover of travel, sports, especially football and basketball.

www.ingramcontent.com/pod-product-compliance
Lightning Source LLC
Chambersburg PA
CBHW061524050726
47503CB00016B/2715